I Will Find You

Douglas Kirk

Imagine, if love could change the past.

Letters to the author should be sent to Morton Falls Publishing Company either by snail mail or e-mail, and, while all cannot be answered, they are encouraged. Readers should send their name, address and e-mail on a picture postcard for notification of other books to be published in this series.

Written by Douglas Kirk
Edited by Lori Kirk
Cover Photo by Douglas Kirk
Cover Design by Kelsie Kirk
Author Photo by Kelsie Kirk

10 9 8 7

Distributed by Morton Falls Publishing Company

ISBN-13: 978-0-934-27917-8
ISBN-10: 0-934279-17-9

Hier ruht in Frieden

LILLY

Tochter von

HERMANN UND EMMA

BARTLES

GEB.

JULI 22, 1894

GEST.

SEPT. 5, 1899

Wenn kleine Himmels erben
In ihrer Unschuld sterben
So büßt man sie nicht ein.

This series is dedicated to *Lilly Bartels*, whose role in a paranormal experience Oct. 24, 2008 at the Startz cemetery, resulted in discussion that lead to the premise of this story.

Chapter 1

October 25, 2008
Canyon Lake, Texas

It was after midnight. Lauri and Wallace had held each other for hours. Their minds were filled with unbelievable possibilities. Thoughts of former lives together were shared without words and exchanged through the warmth of their embrace.

"This is amazing," said Wallace finally.

"I know," replied Lauri softly.

"I feel like I know you, but I don't know you," said the psychologist.

"Me, too," said Lauri.

"How is any of this even possible?"

"I don't know."

"You believe in reincarnation?"

"Do you?" asked Lauri.

"I, don't, I don't know if I do or not. I've never really given it much thought."

"I knew you before. I know I knew you. Don't you feel that?"

"Yes. I do feel it, but why? How?" asked Wallace.

"What about those lives? Why do we know about them? We were them, don't you see? You and I."

"I know," said Wallace, "but I don't get it. I never felt any of that before."

"Until I kissed you," said Lauri.

"But why did you do that? Why would you do that with somebody you've never even seen before?"

"Took a chance, I guess," said Lauri quietly. "You were about to shoot yourself and I didn't know what else to do." She looked into Wallace's brown eyes. They were gentle and understanding.

Wallace examined Lauri's face;

he looked at her lips and chin and at her body. She was such a pretty girl. Her eyes were so expressive and she had such beautiful long blonde hair. He had never seen her before, that's for sure. Yet, he felt connected to her. He had thoughts in his head he had never realized before. But they seemed so real. Previous lives overwhelmed him. Tragedy. Enormous love for this girl. *This* girl.

Where did she come from?

Wallace reached up and stroked Lauri's face slowly.

"You are real," he said. "You really are real. I can't be imagining you."

Lauri kissed him playfully and snapped back.

Wallace smiled.

"Yes, I am real." She smiled. "Either that or you have one heck of an imagination."

Wallace took her hand and looked at it closely. It was dark in the cemetery but he could make out the form. Long, beautiful fingers--so soft, so loving.

By contrast, his hands were larger, and masculine.

"Your hands are familiar," said Lauri after a silence. "I know your hands."

"And I know yours. That's just it," said Wallace, "I know yours. Your hands feel like something I've touched thousands of times. I know I've known you."

Lauri squeezed Wallace's hand. "It's us, don't you see?"

"That's so strange, though," said Wallace. "All those people? We were all those people?"

"No," said Lauri. "No, not all those people. We *are* those two. We are those souls. You and I. Those thoughts, those are memories. We're not imagining this. We're remembering it."

Wallace looked at Lauri's eyes as she spoke. For a moment Wallace and Lauri just looked at each other.

"But how are we communicating?" asked Wallace. "How do we both know the same thing?"

"Our energy is touching. Our auras are the same. Our thoughts are passing back and forth."

"Telepathy?"

"Maybe," said Lauri. "Maybe it is a collective consciousness. We were both there. We've done this before. We never actually died."

"That's a pretty wild thought," said Wallace.

"I know, but do you have a better explanation?"

"I don't have any explanation at all. You found me, remember. I came here to die. You stopped me."

"And aren't you glad?" asked Lauri.

"Yes, I'm glad. Yes, yes. This is amazing. I don't understand it. I have trouble accepting it. But I feel it."

"And I feel it, too," said Lauri.

Wallace looked around the darkened cemetery. The moonlight made the grave markers stand out.

"So all these people aren't dead?" asked Wallace.

"Guess not," said Lauri as she

looked around. "Maybe their bodies are here, but their spirits have traveled on."

"And you and I, what are we, soul mates? M'anamchara?"

"Could be," said Lauri. "Look at what we know about each other and yet we just met. M'anamchara?"

"It's all weird," said Wallace. "Totally strange. M'anamchara is Irish for soul mates."

"We're meant to be?"

"I suppose."

"Why did I get a flat on my car right here where you were about to shoot yourself? If it hadn't been for that flat I would not have stopped. I wouldn't have even seen you. I would have just seen your car and kept going."

"So why did you get the flat?" asked Wallace.

"I don't believe in coincidences."

"So, was it fate?"

"Maybe. How come we keep meeting each other in lifetime after lifetime?"

"You know how crazy that sounds?" asked Wallace.

"Yeah, but so what? We know something. You and I have been together before.

"Can you deny that?"

"Ah," said Wallace. "We just met a couple of hours ago."

"Yes, but what about all that other stuff?"

"Um, it's nuts. It's totally nuts."

"You feel it, though, don't you?"

"Yes," said Wallace.

"Those other lives?"

"Yes."

"How do we even know about that?" asked Lauri.

"Ah, boy. I don't, don't know."

"We lived it. Don't you see? We're still living it. We never died. You and I have been running into each other for hundreds, maybe thousands of years. Don't you feel that?"

"I do feel it," said Wallace, "and that's what's crazy about it."

"Haven't you ever met people before who you instantly liked, and you had this feeling that you knew them somehow?" asked Lauri.

"Yes," agreed Wallace.

"And sometimes you meet people and for no reason you detest them?"

"Yes."

"Well how do you know that something didn't happen in a previous lifetime?"

"I suppose, if you believe in that."

"What? Reincarnation? What's not to believe? If there is an afterlife, why couldn't there be a beforelife?" asked Lauri.

"I hear you. I just never thought it was real. But it sure makes sense."

"So maybe you and I have been lovers for thousands of years and for some reason we keep coming back to each other."

"*Look for me*?" said Wallace slowly.

"*I will find you*," said Lauri softly. "You see, we've both been looking. Ever since the beginning we have had this deal to find each other in the next lifetime."

"Wow," said Wallace. "That just blows my mind."

"Well, me too. But it seems so clear now."

"Really, it does," confirmed Wallace. He looked around again. "So what do we do now?"

Lauri smiled.

"I don't know."

"We sure seem to say that a lot," said Wallace.

"Yeah," smiled Lauri. "We do." She squeezed Wallace's hand. "This is so freaky."

"So you have doubts too?"

"Yes I do, Dub, or whoever you are today."

"Wallace."

"Yeah, I feel that," said Lauri. "This is so totally out of the ordinary."

Wallace laughed out loud. "Like a *lovers'-quarrel-in-the-cemetery-leads-to-50-dead* kind of out of the ordinary?"

"Ha, you caught that."

"Sure, I caught it. It's the real reason I didn't pull the trigger." Wallace looked over at the gun that lay still on the ground. "You just struck me as too funny to take with me into hell."

"Yeah, I didn't want you to do that," said Lauri. "That would have been bad."

"And then you kissed me. Wow! That never happens when a guy is about to off himself."

"Yeah, I know," Lauri said, tilting her head toward the ground, slightly embarrassed. "I don't go around doing that. I can promise you that. I don't know why I did that. It was an impulse."

"Maybe it was just Meallan," said Wallace.

"I guess that has to be it."

The two fell silent once more. Their thoughts raced.

"So what is your name?" asked Wallace finally. "Today, I mean. What do they call you today? I know you went by Meallan and May, and Mary and Misty. Who are you today?"

"Lauri." Lauri extended her hand to formally shake Wallace's hand. They shook. Wallace smiled.

"You're a funny person."

"Got to be," she said. "Life is too

short not to have some fun with it."

"Ha, that's funny," said Wallace, "considering we're sitting here experiencing some kind of connection with our past lives. You know, people talk about past lives and sometimes hypnosis is used to get into that. But this has to be a record."

"What?" asked Lauri.

"This." Wallace pointed back and forth from his body to hers. "This deal here. You know if we tell anybody they will think we are completely smokin' something."

"What?" Lauri said persistently.

"Not only are we claiming past lives, but we are claiming we knew each other in past lives. And, not only that, we knew each other again and again."

"So?"

"So, that's crazy," said Wallace. "I've never even heard of that."

"Sure," said Lauri. "Supposedly certain souls cluster together. It's not all random."

"Whew," breathed Wallace. "This is one for the books." Wallace reached over and cycled the gun. A bullet flipped out onto the ground. "Guess I am not going to use this tonight."

"One bullet?" asked Lauri.

"Right," said Wallace. "It's not too often a guy shoots himself in the head two or three times. It only takes one."

"What if you miss the first shot?"

"Not too likely," he said. "Besides, the first shot either takes you out or turns you into a vegetable."

"Eeuhh, gross."

"I didn't have the nerve to do it anyway."

"That's comforting," said Lauri.

Wallace got up.

"Come on, let's get out of here."

Lauri stood up and tugged Wallace toward her. "What happens now?"

"I guess we go get your tire fixed."

"No, I mean after that?"

"I don't know. We have a heck of a story to tell. You know nobody's going to believe us," said Wallace.

The two walked slowly past the

grave markers and toward Wallace's old gold Mercedes. It was a great car. Wallace had had it a long time and the new models had changed. He liked it because it was fast, yet safe. In his practice he often got called out on emergencies and the car was good because he could get to where he was going quickly. The Mercedes people had engineered it for safety and Wallace liked that about the car, too.

Wallace opened the passenger side door and invited Lauri to take a seat. The keys were still hanging in the ignition.

"You know you should lock your car," said Lauri.

"Why?"

"Well, people could steal it. Do you realize what a significant problem auto theft is?"

Wallace looked at Lauri out of the corner of his eye. He held up the gun.

"Oh," said Lauri, realizing that that would not have mattered had he pulled the trigger and killed himself.

He cranked his engine and looked at Lauri. "Seat belt, please." They both buckled.

Wallace pulled off the side of the road and onto the highway.

"So where's your car?"

"Back the other way."

Wallace slowed and made a three point turn. He drove on past the cemetery toward Lauri's car. "We'll get the wheel and take it in to town to have it fixed. You don't have a spare?"

"I have a spare, but it's flat," said Lauri.

At that instant, there was an enormous smashing noise. Lauri felt pain and passed out suddenly. Wallace saw some kind of flash and went unconscious. There was crumpled metal and smoke and fire. Pieces of another automobile flew in a hundred directions. There was blood splattered inside the car. A man actually crashed through Wallace's front windscreen and plowed into the back seat. Then, except for the sound of fire burning, there was silence.

Chapter 2

October 25, 2008

Cemetery Highway

The view from the AirAmb helicopter was disturbing, even for a veteran pilot and his medical crew. At first it appeared that a single vehicle had exploded. But upon closer examination from above, there was evidence that two vehicles had collided head-on.

One of the vehicles was a Toyota mini-truck and it was pretty much gone. Its pieces were scattered on the highway for a hundred feet in every direction. The only thing discernible about the Mercedes was the passenger module, cocked up toward the sky, with the engine underneath. There was a fire, but it was off to the side of the mass of crumpled metal. Apparently the truck's fuel tank ripped loose and slid into the ditch before it exploded. Had it stayed mounted to the pickup, everything would have been incinerated. A couple of firefighters in yellow bunker gear dragged a hose toward it. A bright light from their fire engine shone on the tank and burned grass was illuminated.

The helicopter circled. There were ambulances with their flashing lights, firefighters standing beside running fire engines, DPS officers, sheriffs' deputies and someone was setting out road flares.

Off in a nearby field the firefighters had set up a landing zone. Flashing strobe lights signaled the pilot where he could safely set down.

The helicopter pilot scanned for telephone lines as he roamed overhead. His machine made a plopping sound. The pilot hovered and looked at the carnage below.

"One DOS," came a calm voice

over the radio. "Two to transport."

The helicopter was generally used to transport one, but two stretchers could be put in through the doors if necessary. It would depend upon the severity of the patients. Sometimes one would be taken on the ground with a box truck and the most critical airlifted to the emergency room by the helicopter.

A paramedic and a nurse on board the chopper would make that determination as soon as they saw the patients themselves.

"White male is in serious condition. Head trauma, difficulty breathing, in and out of consciousness, waiting on vitals," came the voice on the radio. "White female is unconscious, but vitals are stable, she may have internal injuries but she hit an airbag and except for facial lacerations she does not, repeat, does not appear to be bleeding. Her BP is 130 over 78, pulse is 100.

"DOS is a white male, severe head trauma. All are inside the Mercedes. No information on driver of the second vehicle. No information on other possible passengers."

"Copy," said the paramedic inside the helicopter.

"Standby for vitals, adult white male. BP 170 over 102. Pulse 90."

As the helicopter circled again and zeroed in on its makeshift landing zone, the first responders on the ground extracted Lauri from what was left of the Mercedes. She was cold and clammy to the touch. Her pulse was rapid, but weak. Her breathing was shallow.

The men were able to open her crumpled door, but the extraction was slow because the dashboard was pressed against her thighs. They worked furiously to free her and rescue breathing was difficult to administer while she was still trapped inside the car. Finally, she was out. The men carefully lowered her toward the ground. A paramedic squeezed an ambu bag. Lauri's blue jeans had been cut off with bandage scissors and her shirt dangled from a single twist of thread. A hand came out of nowhere to snip it. Her high heels were still on her feet.

The paramedic and an EMT tended to Lauri as three others placed her on a stretcher. They had already put her on a backboard and placed a neck brace on her. An IV line was held high as the workers carefully covered her with a yellow blanket and strapped her to the stretcher with wide orange webbing.

"She's going into shock," said one of the attendants.

"C'mon," said another anxiously.

A firefighter spotted a little flame near the twisted wreck and shot a bit of chemical fire retardant from his extinguisher. A crowd of people worked the other side of the automobile. Some leaned inside the car through the broken windows. Others climbed on the twisted steel. There were lights held up and a firefighter stood by with the Jaws of Life in his hands.

Somebody motioned and the firefighter walked over to the car and climbed a short ladder. He cranked the motor and started working on the hinges of the driver's side door. The noise precluded communication. There were hands everywhere doing their assigned tasks. Orange boxes lay about on the road.

Inside the car was the unforgettable stench of blood and death. The man in the back seat was a mass of flesh. Mixed in was the smell of alcohol.

"That sumbitch is the driver of the other vehicle," announced one of the workers.

"Gahdamn," replied another.

"Poor bastard came in through the front windshield and landed in the back seat." He pointed.

The Jaws of Life snapped off the door and a couple of firefighters handed it away from the wreck.

In the distance, the helicopter motor slowed. The four props were painted red and white, and as they reduced rotation speed, it was easier to see the stripes.

Lauri was on her way to the chopper pushed by a crowd of lifesavers.

The door of the helicopter opened and out popped two men wearing blue flight suits. They looked almost alien. Their helmets made their heads look like that of a dragonfly, with giant eyes and a disproportionate head. One had a large red medical bag slung over his shoulder. It was heavy. He leaned over to the other side pulling against it as he walked. The other man pulled on his green latex gloves while he walked toward the stretcher.

At the wreck, the medics cut the seat belt and gently slid a backboard under Wallace and tied him to it. They had put on the neck support first and had established an IV line where they could push fluids and medications ordered by the doctor at the hospital. They slowly lifted him out of the car. The retrofitted airbag that kept him from plowing into the steering wheel snagged something and one of the responders fought it until it tore.

In the background, Lauri was

loaded into the helicopter as the flight paramedic tended to her.

The man in the back seat was of no concern at that time. His body would be taken out later. Nobody knew who he was. He was unrecognizable. There were beer cans all over the road, though, and the cause of the wreck was pretty clear. He must have been doing a hundred to cause such destruction as he was launched out of his vehicle into the Mercedes driven by Wallace. It was an awful mess.

The helicopter flight to the university hospital was uneventful. AirAmb had done it hundreds of times. The radio traffic was routine. Two were coming into the ER for immediate attention. The trauma surgeon was briefed and the nursing staff was at the ready.

When they arrived, two teams met the helicopter and unloaded first Wallace and then Lauri.

The ER charge nurse directed the operation like a well-oiled watch.

Wallace was conscious at one point, just long enough to look at the crowd of people surrounding him. He wasn't sure where he was or why, but he knew he was in intense pain. Somebody kept talking to him, telling him he was in good hands and he would get the best care and that he would pull through.

Eventually he saw a mask put over his face and that was that.

Wallace awakened hours later in intensive care with two nurses tending to him. He felt light-headed and disoriented.

"Well it looks like you decided to say 'hello'," said a nurse by the name of Sally. She was seasoned, a little odd, but sweet and kind.

"Where am I?" asked Wallace.

"You're on planet Earth," said Sally.

Wallace looked around the ICU.

"Earth?"

"I'm sorry. It's been a long shift. You're at University See Hospital."

"Sea Hospital? Are we at the

ocean?"

"S-e-e. It's a name. University See Hospital."

"That's a stupid name," said Wallace.

"I could not agree with you more." Sally wrote some numbers in Wallace's chart and then punched a computer. "How's your throat?"

"It hurts," said Wallace quietly.

"That's likely from the anesthesia. They put a tube down your throat and that hurts like hell when you wake up."

"I'll say."

"Doctor ordered some meds for pain if you want them."

"What happened?"

"You were in a car accident, you were pretty torn up inside but the surgeon went in and put you back together."

"Where's Meallan?"

"Who?"

"The woman I was with."

"Sir, I think the doctor wants to talk to you about her."

"Is she all right?" asked Wallace.

"I'll let the doctor discuss that with you."

Wallace reached toward the nurse. The pain stopped him.

"She's all right, isn't she?"

Sally looked at Wallace. "She's alive but she's in bad shape. The doctor can tell you more. But for now, you need to be thinking about yourself."

Wallace tried to lean up in bed, but he couldn't. "I don't care about me. I care about her."

"You're both extremely lucky," said Sally.

"I don't feel lucky."

"Your doctor is the best in the business. The best. You're going to hurt for awhile, but you're going to walk away from this thing. The paramedic told the staff the car was totaled."

"What happened?" asked Wallace.

"Don't know for sure," said Sally as she adjusted the blanket on Wallace's bed. "The ER staff said it was a head-on. You're lucky to be alive."

Wallace licked his lips.

"Are you thirsty?" asked Sally.

"Yeah," whispered Wallace. He closed his eyes.

"We'll get something for you."

Hospitals are not a place to rest and intensive care is the most active unit in any hospital, secondary only to the ER. Time crawls for the patient. There are hours of boredom punctuated with noise, beepers going off, nurses fiddling with equipment and typing into computers, handing over medication, and there are bright lights. There are way too many bright lights.

Wallace slept some, but spent a lot of time trying to put the pain out of his mind. They gave him drugs. He had all kinds of things poured into his system. He complained of the pain; they said they gave him something to "take the edge off" but he openly wondered if it was some kind of Nazi experiment gone bad.

The nurses were pleasant enough, but when pain rules, every

nurse seems like Nurse Ratched, and every pill seems like a placebo.

To Wallace it seemed like a hundred years before the doctor showed up.

The doctor was dressed in surgical greens, kind of squat, with a pooch belly and a little bit of gray hair protruding from his scrub cap. After looking at the chart, he told Wallace that he was doing great. Wallace didn't feel so great, but after listening to the doctor describe his internal injuries he started to understand.

The impact of the pickup hitting the Mercedes tore some of his organs from their attachments. There was a rip in the liver, which was repaired by the surgery, and except for losing a lot of blood and receiving a lot of blood, Wallace was in pretty good shape. It would take awhile to heal, but he'd pull through.

"So how did all this happen?" asked Wallace.

The surgeon stood next to the bed and looked at each of Wallace's eyes as a nurse stood by.

"Car accident," he said finally. "You came in after a head-on collision. One died."

Wallace felt a sense of panic when he heard that last two words. The doctor kept talking, but Wallace didn't hear anything after that.

"What? Wait. Who died?" asked Wallace.

"Evidently it was the man that hit you," said the doctor.

Wallace was sad, but relieved.

"What about Lauri?"

"The woman with you, is that your daughter? Your wife?"

"Sister-in-law," said Wallace slowly. "How is she?"

The doctor looked at Wallace briefly and then answered in a monotone.

"We're working on her. She's in a coma. She appears to be healing up okay, didn't really have much wrong with her. Some scrapes on her face where the airbag hit her. Minor injuries to her legs. But she's not coming out of it."

"What?" asked Wallace. His mind reeled. He rubbed at some of the bandages on his face and head.

"Sometimes that happens," said the doctor. "Brain swelling is pretty bad with her. We're watching her very closely. Somebody is with her around the clock."

"What's wrong with her?" asked Wallace as if he had not heard the doctor's explanation.

"Trauma to the head," said the doctor. "We're running tests. The neurologist has her listed as a 5T."

"What does that mean?" asked Wallace.

"On the Glasgow Coma Scale she's a 5T. That's pretty serious. She could go either way."

"What do you mean 'either way'?"

"Sometimes patients get worse and they come down on the scale. Any lower and she might not recover. If she goes up the scale, there's hope."

Wallace looked at the doctor silently.

"The organ recovery coordinator

is on his way over," continued the doctor.

"What?" said Wallace with shock.

"It's required. Any patient with a 5 or below and we have to call the coordinator."

"She could die?" asked Wallace.

"Yes, but we are not giving up on her. If we get the swelling in her cranium under control, she could recover."

"Where is she?" asked Wallace.

"She's here in the hospital."

"I want to see her," said Wallace assertively. He moved as though he wanted to get up. The doctor and the nurse both put their hands on him to encourage him to sit back.

"You don't want to be moving right now," said the doctor.

"Where is she? Is she in a room?"

"She's in the neuro ICU on the third floor," said the doctor. "We will keep you posted. You are in no condition to be moving around, and she's unconscious."

"She needs to hear my voice," said Wallace instinctively.

"In time," said the doctor. "You stay right here. These nurses are going to take care of you. We are going to take care of her. Just as soon as we can, we will let you see her. But not now."

Wallace sighed, leaned back and closed his eyes. What the hell, he thought. There's always something.

In the neuro ICU, the organ recovery coordinator had just arrived. Richard Strain was a legend in his own right, an RN, but skilled with organs in ways even doctors envied.

With 40 years of transplant experience under his belt, he was the expert. Bald and smiling, he was fit and rugged, 5 feet 9 inches tall. He had an engaging smile and a handsome complexion.

All the staff knew him. He was a talker, for sure, with one of the toughest jobs in the world. If a person was in a coma and death could result, his job was to speak to the family and coordinate the use of the organs to save other lives. His first ever heart transplant was an absolute miracle. The first pediatric heart transplant on record, in the 1980s, the organ was placed in an ice chest and doctors flew with it to the hospital where they could place it in another child's chest. The boy was 11 and lived to 21--unheard of at the time.

When Richard first met the mother of the unfortunate child who had been injured in a BB gun accident, the first thing she said was, "I know who you are and why you are here." She had had a dream about it. She said that God had told her this would happen. Richard replied to her that he hoped God had given some details because it was all untried and he wasn't sure how he was going to find a recipient in time, or where. Kidneys had been placed in ice and flown to distant locations for implant--successfully, but never a heart. Heart transplants in adults had been done before, but only from one surgical suite to the adjoining one. Distance meant time, and time was believed to be the limiting factor.

Richard then spent the next 27

hours on the phone finding a recipient. When he finally found one, way before the days of computer matching, the woman on the phone hollered, "He's got the heart!" Then, when Richard talked to the surgeon, the doctor initially said "no" because the distance was just too far. It had never been attempted. But Richard re-phoned him all night long until he said "yes." He was persistent, and as the doctor's own patient deteriorated, the surgeon agreed to try it.

It was the start of saving a lot of lives. It had never been done before, but after Richard Strain proved it could be successful, he was the go-to-guy who moved the organs across the country from hospital to hospital. He landed on runways much too short for a Lear jet, saving lives like it was meant to be. Over his lifetime, he saved thousands.

Richard looked at Lauri. The long vehicle extraction had caused hypoxia. She should have been ventilated faster and more thoroughly. She was in bad shape, with a brain much larger than normal, swelling, pushing down on the brain stem. It was an uncal herniation. Sometimes patients recover from that. Sometimes they don't. It was to be a wait and see game. A hard game. She was a 5T. That's bad. If she dropped on the scale and landed at 3T, her organs could be harvested. If she went the other way, she could live. Time would tell.

Richard studied Lauri. He felt he knew her. He wasn't sure, but he felt something. He couldn't quite place his feelings as he stood looking at her in the bed with all the equipment keeping her alive. One of the nurses noticed him gazing at her but did not interrupt. Then, he pursed his lips and abruptly turned. There was other work to do. He walked away.

Chapter 3

October 29, 2008

San Antonio, Texas

It was several days before the doctor let the staff roll Wallace in a wheelchair down to the third floor to see Lauri. He had been moved to a room somewhere in the hospital labyrinth and his persistent requests to see Lauri were finally rewarded. His hair was tossed and twisted and he wore one of those ugly hospital gowns with no back. Some of the bandages had been removed from his face and the bruises and scabs were anything but handsome.

Wallace's heart sank when he saw Lauri. She looked extremely pale and her face was thin and unresponsive. She had a massive bruise on her face and some lacerations that had scabbed over.

Wallace had only just met Lauri but during the little time he spent with her, she was so full of life. To see her hooked up to a mass of machines was disheartening.

"Oh, my God," Wallace whispered as the aide pushed him up to Lauri's bed. His mind galloped. "Oh, jeez," he said.

"Excuse me?" asked the woman.

"Nothing," said Wallace. "Is this the way she's been?"

"Sir, I haven't been in here myself."

At that, one of the nurses working the unit stepped past the long white curtain that hung from the ceiling.

"Are you Wallace Larame? The one who's been asking about her?"

"Yes," said Wallace.

"I'm Nurse Fields and she is doing very well--under the circumstances. All her vitals are good. She's been run through a lot of tests. They've upgraded her to a 7T on the Glasgow." The nurse paused. "What is she to you, Mr. Larame? You came into the ER together but you have different last names."

"How do you know her name?" asked Wallace.

"The police located her car not far from the accident and they got her purse and driver's license from the car," said Nurse Fields.

"Sister-in-law," said Wallace. He didn't even know her last name himself, but was not about to describe the circumstances wherein they met.

"Is she sleeping?" asked Wallace.

"No, she's still in a coma. She has been unconscious, I guess since the accident. But she is in very good shape."

"How do you mean?"

"Well," said the nurse, a slim, middle-aged woman with years of experience, "except for the coma, she's great."

"Isn't that odd?" asked Wallace.

"Well, not really. Depends upon what is causing the coma. Might be just swelling from the trauma."

"What do the doctors say?"

"Well, they haven't really. They don't know exactly what is going on. They thought maybe an aneurysm, but they didn't pick up anything on the CAT scan."

"Is her brain working?"

"Yes, yes. She's normal. It's just that she is comatose. She is doing much better than when she came in, but she has a long way to go."

Wallace looked at Lauri and reached his hand over to pat her arm, which was tucked under the sheet.

"So what happens now?" asked Wallace.

"We wait."

At that, Dr. Rogers stepped into the area. He was a very tall man, almost like a basketball player. He had a head full of red hair and he sported rosy cheeks.

"Are you Wallace Larame?" asked the doctor.

"Yes," said Wallace.

"I'm Dr. Rogers. We've been working with Lauri very closely. From the way I hear it, you two are very lucky to be alive. "

"Why is she in a coma?" asked Wallace.

"Good question," answered the doctor. "I'm not sure that I know the answer to that. She is doing extremely well. Her injuries from the accident are healing nicely. And she didn't really have many. The airbag tore her face up a little. But internally we've found nothing wrong. Her brain is swollen, so I am thinking trauma to the brain put her in the coma. We've looked at the scans and the neurologist can't find anything major and I can't see anything. I've ordered some more tests. We're just going to have to keep looking. I'm giving her medication to reduce the swelling."

Wallace gripped Lauri's arm and worked down to her hand.

"Why would swelling make her go into a coma?" asked Wallace.

"Well it doesn't always," said Dr. Rogers. "Sometimes in a severe auto accident the head is kicked back and forth and that jostles the brain inside the cranium. That causes swelling and the swelling can push down on the reticular activating system--that's part of the old brain, what they call the rhinencephalon. With that pressure the RAS can sometimes shut down the consciousness. We are assisting her breathing but her heart works fine by itself. It is like being asleep. But we can't wake her. The coma determines her level of consciousness."

"I see," said Wallace. "So the accident is what caused it?"

"Well, we think. I looked at the other possibilities, blood sugar, say if she were diabetic, drugs or other toxins. I looked at her electrolytes and hormones, sometimes they can get out of balance and cause a coma. There wasn't any serious bleeding. I don't think she has had a stroke or an aneurysm. This gal just took a hell of a knock on the head. You can see where the airbag tore up her face. So think about that. First her head moves forward suddenly when the vehicles initially hit and then, the airbag blows and throws her head back. It could just be trauma from that. I'm looking at all the possibilities."

"Can she hear us?" asked Wallace.

"Well, that's what the experts say. There is nothing wrong with her senses. I don't see anything wrong with her brain *per se*. Chances are if you talk to her she will hear what you have to say."

"Maybe that will help her," said Wallace.

"I'm optimistic that it will," said the doctor. "Who's your doctor?"

"I don't know," said Wallace apologetically. "There have been a bunch of people. He told me but I don't remember."

"That's okay," said Dr. Rogers. "I'll send instructions to the staff on your floor to bring you down here a couple of times per day."

"Why can't I just stay?"

"No," said the doctor, "there are a lot of other patients they're caring for here and you need to not be here most of the time, scheduled visits only."

"Can she be moved to a room?"

"No, I want her here where the nurses can be right with her. Look, I'll have you brought down here three times per day for an hour each visit."

"Okay," said Wallace as he looked back at Lauri.

"I'll be checking in on her, and I've asked Dr. Rigdon from Austin to consult on the case. He's a neurosurgeon who specializes in traumatic brain injuries. I've talked to him on the phone and he will be here tomorrow to examine her and look at the records. Lauri's prognosis is very optimistic. We just need to be patient and keep treating her and keep on top of it."

"Okay, thank you, doctor."

"I'll be in and out. I'll let you know if anything develops."

As quick as he had arrived, Dr. Rogers disappeared. Wallace heard him telling the nurse at the desk to let him stay an hour and then let him visit three times per day.

Wallace looked at Lauri. She had not moved. Her respirations were deep and regular. The ventilator made a barely audible hissing sound.

Wallace looked around the cubicle and he scanned the machines that were hooked up to Lauri. He could see her heartbeat on the monitor. There was an indication of her breathing, and a blood pressure readout. He watched her lay there.

"Meallan," he said in a low voice finally, "It's me. I'm here. Can you hear me? I'm so sorry. I didn't even see the vehicle coming. I'd do anything to trade places with you right now."

Wallace looked around the neuro ICU. There were beepers and lights and a couple of nurses whisked by in a hurry to do something.

"Meallan. Lauri. We just got together and it can't end like this. You have to be strong. You have to fight this. I know you can hear me. You have to come back to me. Lauri?"

Wallace pulled the sheet down a little so that he could grasp her hand with both of his. She felt warm but there was no return to the grip.

He wondered if that is what it would be like if she died. Warm at first, but then, gradually, growing colder.

He didn't like that thought and he fought to put it out of his mind.

"We found each other," he said softly. "After all this time, we found each other. It can't end like this."

Chapter 4

February 14, 1898

Los Angeles, California

Mary had not seen her son in years and she missed him. He had moved away from California to pursue his dream and wound up working for the *New York Empire* as a reporter. At the age of 28, he had been promoted to the position of headline writer for foreign correspondence, a pretty responsible job for one of the largest newspapers in the country.

It was the heyday of yellow journalism. Facts were not to interfere with a good story and the war frenzy that was going on over Spain's control of Cuba made for good copy. The people who ran the newspapers were in brutal competition with one another and if an exaggerated headline could sell more newspapers than the competition, then a wild headline was considered a good thing. Sometimes stories were completely fabricated. Sometimes they were rewritten to sound better than they really were.

But nobody was checking and when one paper broke and misrepresented a story, the others had to follow suit by writing something even more dramatic.

The paper boys sold copies on the street based upon the headlines and so everyone was part of the game. The goal was to sell a million copies each and every day.

Darin was a spitting image of his father, with wavy hair and a smile that made people feel good. He was thin, about 5 feet 11 inches, and he walked with dispatch. While he did not care much for the whole yellow journalism scene, he was caught up in it. How could he not be? It was an exciting time in New York City and for a man of Irish descent to have control over what the people of New York were to read, it was pretty heady.

Mary had carried her age well, now 48. She hardly ever cut her hair and it was straight and beautiful, a sort of dirty blonde. Her eyes were blue as ice and stunning from a distance, incredible up close. She had abandoned the name of Hillten and had taken Connors, though she never divorced the first, nor married the second man in her life. She figured Clarence Hillten probably hunted for her, but with the name of Connors, the name of the man he likely murdered, Hillten never found her or her son.

Darin had just come back to New York from a trip to Cuba and while it was uncertain and dangerous work, he loved it. He had been sent to uncover Spanish atrocities, to chase a story of cannibalism, to get the goods on the torture of Cuban rebel prisoners. The Cuban nationals were trying to throw off the bondage of Spain, and America was taking a front seat to help them.

Mary finally decided to visit after years of making plans, and so she was on her way by train.

The passenger car was crowded. A lot of people made the trip from California to New York in those days and the country was bustling with activity. The steam engine pulled out of the station precisely at 8:00 am and chugged its way up over the mountains. Mary watched through the window as the majestic iron horse spewed a long cloud of white steam. The noise disrupted the birds that had perched in nearby trees. Choosh, choosh, choosh, went the engine as the cars groaned against gravity. The engine pulled them up the steep grade.

Mary looked out over the valley on the winter day. It wasn't cold. There was a nip in the air, but nothing unpleasant. The sun was shining.

Mary realized it was Valentine's Day. She had not thought so intensely about Darby for awhile, but Valentine's

Day always made her daydream about him. He was a real man. He stood up for men. He fought for men. He would have been proud of their son, a newspaper man. Darby couldn't read and yet his son was making a living writing. Mary made sure of that. Anybody with the heritage of Darby Connors would be a champion for people and she knew from early on that her son would be that kind of man.

As she left LA behind her, Mary thought briefly about the message she was bringing to Darin. It was much too personal to write in a letter over long distance, and so she was resigned to visit him and tell him in person. It was a decision that she had taken years to reach, but once made, she wanted to tell him face-to-face. She hoped he would take it well. He was a good boy and he respected his mother. She was getting older and certain things needed to happen--at least, that's what she felt.

Mary looked out over the landscape. Amazing, she thought, how life goes sometimes. You can't tell what lies in store ahead and it's funny how one day can make all the difference in the world. She smiled to herself. She had been alone for so many years that she could carry on both sides of a conversation in her head. She was happy. And she was sad. She missed Darby. Oh, how she missed Darby.

One night together and she had a wonderful son. But Darby wasn't there to enjoy it. He wasn't there to enjoy her. And he wasn't there for her. How she wished he was there. How she missed him so very much.

The conductor spoke twice before Mary looked up.

"Tickets. Ticket please."

Mary looked up from her thoughts.

"I'm sorry," she said. "What?"

"May I see your ticket please?" said the conductor.

Mary dug in her bag for the ticket and handed it over. The man punched it and moved along. "Tickets. Ticket please," he said to the next passenger. The Central Pacific Railroad was efficient. Mary wondered, had Darby worked on this rail line? She smiled. Darby Connors.

What would he think about the way the unions had organized the coal mines and the steel mills and the railroads and every other industry in America? He was among the first to fight for the rights of the workers and though he was murdered for his efforts, the efforts had succeeded.

Mary rode the train first to Sacramento and then east all day and on into the night, and all the next day until they finally reached Promontory Summit, Utah. The train stopped there to take on supplies and passengers and Mary walked about the station made famous by the "Golden Spike", where the Central Pacific Railroad and Union Pacific Railroad came together in the great race across the country. Hundreds of miles of tracks were laid, one ten mile stretch was laid in a single day. In a hurry to gobble up territory, the rail lines were awarded sections of land all along the line, ten square miles of land for every mile of track laid--33 million acres in all. It had been a grand project and now Mary could get from California to New York in four days, four hours and forty minutes.

By nightfall on February 15, she was pretty tired and while it is hard to sleep in coach, she was so weary that she did.

In New York City, news of the sinking of the *USS Maine* came as a shock. It happened at 9:40 pm, February 15, 1898.

The US battleship had been sent to Havana a few weeks before to protect Americans, to encourage the Cuban rebels and to dissuade the Spanish. But there wasn't much of a war going on, and the Captain of the Maine found the Spanish to be hospitable and there wasn't much chance of conflict.

That his ship was blown out from under him was a shock. He had been in his stateroom writing in his journal when he heard the explosion and felt the ship list. He wrote later that his first thought was about his own personal safety but his training as a leader took over. One third of the forward part of the ship had been blown up and within moments it sank to the bottom of the harbor, leaving the bridge visible above sea level. As many as 254 men perished that night, 59 were wounded and eight died later on shore.

A Spanish ship came to the rescue and while the event was later investigated, it was never really clear if a mine was detonated, if a powder magazine on board exploded; whether it was an accident or an act of war.

But the papers in New York really didn't need the facts. Spain was blamed and the Hearsts and the Pulitzers and all the other big newspaper owners were on the warpath. America would go to war over the incident and there was no stopping it.

Daniel banged on Darin's door as hard as he could. Darin had already gone to bed when the wire of the explosion reached New York and Darin was needed to write the headlines for a special edition.

Daniel was his contemporary, same age, same job, same laughs. They were best of friends and Daniel lived just a few doors down in the same apartment building. Daniel was different though, mature beyond his years, quick witted and smart. Everyone looked up to him, including Darin. They were lucky to know each other, because neither had any siblings and both considered the other like a brother. Daniel was a little taller than Darin, with a head full of sandy hair and a perpetual grin.

"Darin!" shouted Daniel. "Get up. Got to go to work. There's been an explosion!"

Darin cracked open the door. "What? You want to wake up the whole building?"

"It's the news! The Spanish sank the *Maine*."

"What?" asked Darin as he pulled open the door.

Daniel rushed in. "Got to get

going, buddy. The Spanish bombed the *Maine* and it is sitting at the bottom of the harbor!"

"Holy smoke!" said Darin. "How do we know?"

"It's on the wire. We're going to need to reset the front page and print a special edition."

"Dang," said Darin as he fumbled with his trousers. "I can't believe they did that."

"That's what they're saying. Witnesses say there was a big fireball. The explosion knocked out all the glass in the buildings around there. Sailors were swimming. And get this: The Spanish themselves sent a vessel over to rescue the survivors."

"They blow it up and then help out?" asked Darin.

"That's what they're saying."

"I can't believe it."

"Get some headlines cookin' because this is big news."

"All right, what about '*Maine Is Blown Up In Havana Harbor*'?" Darin gestured with his hands to show the type would run all across the page.

"Second line, all caps, but smaller, *'America's Battleship Destroyed'.*"

"Was it destroyed?" asked Darin.

"I don't know," said Daniel. "They say she's sitting on the bottom. I'd say that is destroyed."

"All right, third line, *'All Killed, No Survivors.'* Were there any survivors?"

"I don't know," said Daniel. "We're trying to find out."

"There had to be survivors," reasoned Darin. "If the Spanish ship rescued some of them then there had to be survivors. So we go with, *'Many Are Reported Either Killed or Hurt.'*"

"You're the best," said Daniel. "Come on, hurry up."

Darin grabbed a shirt and the two bolted out the door.

They lived downtown Manhattan so the newspaper office was not far away and they decided it would be quickest to jog to it.

The *New York Empire* was bustling with activity. There were only about a million telephones in the United States in 1898, but it seemed on the night the *Maine* went down, all of them were ringing. The telegraph machines were spitting out copy and reporters in Havana were digging up as much information as they could.

In New York, the copywriters at every paper were busy weaving their yarns while press operators stood by to run the new front pages. This news would sell and it would sell big.

The typesetters reached for their largest type--carved wooden letters seldom used. EXTRA was carefully centered at the top of the galley. Upside down and backwards was the way the type was laid in place, one letter at a time.

Darin scribbled some more headlines: "*Disaster Occurs While Crew Is Fast Asleep. Wounded Survivors Are Unable To Explain The Terrible Affair.*"

As the bits and pieces of the story came in, Darin wrote more: "*All The*

Boats Of The Spanish Cruiser Alfonzo XII Are Sent To The Assistance Of The Officers And Crew Of The Wrecked Vessel."

Daniel stood and looked over his shoulder. "That's good." Daniel yelled the new headline material to the typesetter at the other end of the room, who composed it on the fly.

It was exciting. Breaking news was going directly to type and in minutes off to the printer.

They labeled the top of the paper, *"3:30 A.M."* in an effort to beat the other papers that would be on the street at the same time.

The rest of the paper had already been composed the night before and there was no time to make any changes. The *EXTRA* edition would go out and sell fast. Then, as quickly as it was to be sent out, the regular paper would be adapted to detail the news and the new stories.

Daylight came before they knew it. It was a labor they all loved and by the time New Yorkers were on their way to work, the *New York Empire* would have two editions on the street, the *3:30 A.M. EXTRA* and the regular morning edition as a follow-up. There would be big money made--twice as many papers sold. Bad news is always good for the news business.

In a small coffee shop near the newspaper office, Darin and Daniel sat together after the work was done.

"Good job," Daniel said to Darin. "Good job by everybody."

A paperboy could be heard outside the shop yelling, "Extra, extra, *Spanish Armada Sinks USS Maine.*"

Darin shook his head and laughed. He knew that that's the way the news would be sold.

"You know my mom is coming in this week," said Darin.

"Yeah, that's what you said."

"I haven't seen her in five years," said Darin. "She's getting up in the years. I hope I recognize her."

Daniel laughed. "You'll recognize her, she's your mother. You'll always recognize her."

Darin smiled. "We did a good job today."

"Yes, we did." Daniel clinked his coffee cup against Darin's.

Mary heard about the bombing of the *USS Maine* that next morning on the train. There were a couple of papers people brought on board at one of the stops but the information was sketchy. The news worried Mary. Darin had written her that he had gone down to Cuba and she was afraid that if a war broke out he'd be going again. It was a long journey to New York, but the worry made it longer.

Darin and Daniel took the trolley over to the train station to meet Mary when she arrived two days later. Darin spotted her immediately as she climbed off the coach with a small bag and an umbrella. Daniel noticed her eyes and was taken by them. She was a striking woman and he couldn't resist saying so.

"You are every bit as beautiful as

your son let on," said Daniel graciously when he was introduced by Darin as Daniel McGinty, best friend, co-worker and mentor.

"Why, thank you," said Mary. She smiled and turned toward her son adoringly.

"*The Most Terrific Mother In The World*," said Darin as he wrote the words in the air. He hugged her and held her tight.

Mary chuckled. "I see you're still writing headlines for that newspaper of yours."

Daniel laughed. "He is the best in the business."

"Mom, do you have a trunk?"

"Yes," said Mary. "It's not big, but you boys will have to carry it for me."

The three walked off the platform toward the freight office. It would be awhile before the freight and luggage were unloaded, so they decided to sit inside. The laborers had already started removing the luggage and placing it on large steel-wheeled carts.

As Mary sat visiting with Darin, Daniel found himself looking at her closely. A time or two she noticed and he broke off his stare. Then, he noticed her looking at him. It was strange. One time Daniel just smiled and tried to make small talk.

"So how was the trip over?"

"Uneventful," said Mary.

The three laughed a little.

"Uneventful. That's good," said Daniel.

Darin held his hands up as if scribing a headline.

"Woman From California Says Trip to New York Uneventful."

They laughed in earnest.

"It's funny about the news," said Daniel a little more seriously. "They never report how many people did not get injured today, or how many people were not sick, or which banks were not robbed."

"That's true," said Mary. "I'd like to see a newspaper publish that."

"But then nobody would buy it," said Darin. "If it isn't dramatic, it doesn't sell."

"But that's important. When people don't get hurt, isn't that important?" asked Mary.

"Sure it is," said Daniel.

"But nobody will pay to read that," said Darin.

The trolley trip back to downtown was fascinating for Mary. She had never been to New York and while she was used to Los Angeles, she certainly never expected the buildings to be so tall and the streets so crowded. New York City was certainly filled with activity and she caught herself marveling at just about everything.

Daniel watched her with fascination. He and Darin knew all about the city, being in the newspaper business, but Daniel was surprised at how filled with joy Mary was. Everything seemed to excite her. An old tenement building spurred a lot of questions. The number of motorcars caught her attention. The people, so many people on their way to somewhere--she commented on that.

Darin smiled the whole way. It was good to have his mother visit and he was pleased that she would be staying with him for an undetermined amount of time.

Daniel answered her questions and she liked that he seemed to enjoy pointing out the sights. Her son had chosen his friend well, she thought, as they came to the stop near the boys' apartment.

Darin muscled Mary's trunk off the trolley while Daniel offered his hand and helped his friend's mother to the street. He carried her bag and her umbrella with a certain playful authority. He directed Darin to hold the trunk well up off the pavement and to make sure he didn't hit the bottom of a window canopy.

Mary laughed at the boys' antics and enjoyed them doting over her.

Inside the building, up a couple of flights of stairs, Daniel walked them to Darin's door and bade them goodbye.

"Well, he is quite an interesting man," said Mary as Darin closed the apartment door. "And handsome, too."

Mary looked around the apartment. It was small. It was very small. The apartment consisted of a bathroom, a walk-in closet and a bigger room divided by a short wall, half the kitchen, half the bedroom.

Mary looked around at the stacks and stacks of newspapers and books. They were everywhere.

Darin noticed her looking and so he quickly started straightening up.

Mary put her hand on his forearm to stop him.

"You're my son," she said. "You don't have to impress me."

Darin smiled and set a stack of papers back on a small table.

"Besides," she said, "once you pick up a pile of these things, just what do you intend to do with them?"

Darin burst out laughing. He hugged his mother.

"It's good to see you, Mom."

"You're my boy," she said. "And I love you so much."

"Me too," said Darin. He stepped

back and gestured at the room. "It's pretty small, but I'm seldom here."

Mary smiled. "It looks like you never leave. You certainly never leave with anything in your hands. It all comes in and nothing goes out."

Darin grinned and looked at the floor.

Mary picked up a newspaper. "But you can read. Do you know how important that is? Not only can you read, but you make a living writing. Your father would have been so proud of you."

Darin moved a couple of things off the couch, a sort of divan that turned into a bed.

"Sit down," he invited.

Mary sat. "I love what you've done with your apartment."

Darin looked around with a puzzled smile on his face. Mary burst out laughing and Darin chuckled.

"Well, yes, it could use a mother's touch."

Mary smiled. "Oh, no. This is yours. This is your personality. You are so filled with ideas and you are so much a part of the city."

"Yeah," said Darin. "Yeah, it's great living and working here."

"Your father would be so proud."

"You said that," said Darin.

"He would. I know you never knew him, but he lived in an apartment much like this one. In fact, I think you both have the same decorator."

Darin snickered. "What was he like, Mom?"

Mary looked at her son with a serious face.

"He was a wonderful man. He was a man who led others and fought for others, and helped others. He is the reason you are in this country, the reason you are American."

"He emigrated from Ireland?" asked Darin.

"Yes, yes he did. Proud and strong. He worked his way over with nothing in his pockets. He had a strong back and a strong will, like so many of the Irish."

"And what did he do?" asked

Darin, about his father.

"What didn't he do?" said Mary. "He was a railroad worker for almost twenty years. He built rail tracks across this country. And when he finished that work, he went to work in the coal mine in Pennsylvania to put fuel in the steam engines."

"That's where you met him?" asked Darin.

"Yes it is."

"How?" asked Darin.

"I worked in the office. I met him the day he applied for a job. And I knew then that there was something special about him. I knew then that he would be an important man."

"Didn't he start the union there?"

"Yes he did," said Mary.

"And that's how he died?"

"Yes," Mary said slowly, "yes, it is. They said it was an accident, but we all know it wasn't."

"Why?" asked Darin with a little tear sliding onto his cheek.

"They wanted to stop him so that they could stop the union."

"Didn't work, did it?" asked Darin.

"No it didn't. It did not work. And that old mean boss that ran that mine disappeared and died for all we know." Mary paused. "And they got their union. The mine closed but the union grew. Your father saved a lot of lives because of what he did. He saved a lot of children from dying in those wretched mines."

"You loved him a lot, didn't you?" said Darin.

"With all my heart," said Mary as she turned and looked out the window. "I love him with all my heart."

"I'm sorry, Mom," said Darin.

"It's all right. It was a long time ago."

Darin walked into the kitchen. "Do you want something to drink?"

Mary smiled. "You're just like your father." She tilted her head down.

"Why do you say that?" asked Darin.

"You just are. Be proud of that. Your father was a good man."

At that, a knock was on the door.

Darin hurried to open it. "I've asked Daniel to have supper with us."

Mary stood up and wiped a tear from her eye and straightened her dress.

"Are you cooking?"

"No," said Darin. "This is a special occasion and we are going to a very special restaurant."

"We don't have..." said Mary.

"Yes we do," said Darin, interrupting.

Daniel popped through the open door. "I am ready to go," he announced.

"That didn't take you long," said Mary.

"I am always ready to go," replied Daniel. "You mention food and I am ready to do my share for the American farmer."

"I don't know about you," said Darin jokingly. "A guy like you eats so much food there are people starving because of it."

"On the contrary," quipped Daniel, "I provide steady employment for the farmers so that they can grow their food with confidence that there will be a market."

Mary looked at the two and shook her head. She stepped into the bathroom and closed the door.

"Sorry," said Daniel.

"No, no problem. My mom likes to joke. She's very witty."

"I noticed that about her." Daniel leaned toward Darin. "She sure is young," he whispered. "She's not like anybody else's mother I've ever met."

"Yeah," said Darin, "she's something else."

Daniel looked around the apartment.

"So where's she going to sleep?"

"I'm giving her my bed. I'm sleeping in the closet," said Darin.

A huge grin came across Daniel's face. "I tell you. You are the one who is something else."

"It will work. It won't be that hot."

Daniel laughed. "Why don't you come down and stay with me and let her have your place to herself?"

Darin considered the idea. "Maybe. We'll see what she prefers."

Supper was entertaining. The three walked to an Italian restaurant, looked at the menu and then left for something more in keeping with Irish taste. At another place, they ate fried steaks and potatoes and carrots. It was pretty good stuff, all considered, and the evening was fun.

A time or two Daniel noticed Mary looking at him and their eyes caught. Daniel felt a little embarrassed by it but he couldn't help himself. He was drawn to Mary. He found himself, a time or two, wishing Darin wasn't there. Mentally, he shook himself.

Chapter 5

February 1898

New York, New York

Over the next several days the war news heated up. The *New York Empire* was competing with the other papers, stirring anti-Spanish sentiment and calling for outright Cuban revolt.

Darin and Daniel were busy. The job was demanding and when the news unfolded, the newspapermen were hard at work. Cuban revolutionaries had been trying to win independence from Spain since 1895, and the sinking of the *Maine* was just the event they needed to call attention to Spanish atrocities and spur America into action.

It was not clear who actually bombed the *Maine*, but regardless, the newspapers squarely blamed Spain.

The Democrats pressed Republican William McKinley to go to war, on the one hand to help the Cubans, and on the other, to blame McKinley for a war. American merchant ships had trouble completing their trade missions to Cuba and the economic impact was cited as a key reason to enter a war with Spain. Some called for American expansionism and imperialism around the world, citing a powerful Navy as the means to accomplish foreign influence. Every move made for huge headlines and all the New York newspapers sold large numbers of each edition. It was yellow journalism at its finest and Daniel and Darin were in the big middle of it.

Over the coming days, Mary enjoyed New York City and took the time by herself to travel about and see the sights.

She wanted to visit Ellis Island,

the first federal immigration station in the nation, but there were no ferries carrying sightseers out to the island after the terrible fire that destroyed the original three story wooden structure on June 15, 1897. Millions of immigrants had been processed through the facility during its first five years of operation, but the fire of unknown origin put a stop to that--at least until it could be rebuilt. In its place workers were building a giant red brick structure--indestructible, they said.

Mary was interested in seeing Ellis Island because she believed Darby had told her he entered the country through New York. She remembered he once told her that it was terrible having to sleep out in the cold, listening to people snore and dream in a dozen languages.

As she read about it though, she realized that Ellis Island was not even in operation when he arrived, and that he probably came in through Castle Garden at the Battery in lower Manhattan--which is where so many landed after the Atlantic crossing.

After a long day in the city, Mary found herself sitting in Darin's apartment rubbing her feet. There was a knock on the door.

"Who is it?" she asked with a slightly raised voice.

"It's me, Daniel."

Mary slipped on her shoes.

"Just a minute please."

She went to the door to see Daniel with a look of anxiety on his face.

"What's wrong?" she asked instinctively.

"May I come in?" Daniel replied.

"Sure," said Mary, "where's Darin?"

"He's on his way to the train station. They are sending him to Cuba again and he asked me to pick up a few things for him."

"Why?" asked Mary.

"I guess he needed them," said Daniel.

"No, why are they sending him to Cuba?"

"I guess they wanted the best reporters in the field. He writes headlines that sell papers and they want him down there to see the revolt first hand. Makes for better headlines."

Mary's heart dropped.

"I don't want him going to the war," said Mary clearly.

"No choice," said Daniel. "Besides, it's safe."

"No war is safe," said Mary with concern. She had been very young, but the memory and the horror of the Civil War was still with her.

Daniel dug around in Darin's closet and found a canvas bag Darin had used on his previous trip.

"Why him?" asked Mary.

"He's the best," Daniel called out. "They only send the best." Daniel scampered around the apartment gathering clothes and some other things Darin had requested.

Mary sat at the table and scribbled a note to her son. She wrote furiously while Daniel stuffed clothing in the bag. She had not wanted to tell

Darin the news in a letter, but now there was a chance he would not return home before she had to go back to California.

Mary was upset and it showed. Inside, she was scared for her son and while it was a huge adventure for him, any mother would worry.

As Daniel was about to leave, Mary folded the piece of paper and handed it to him.

"Give this to Darin, please," she said. "I came to New York to give him some news and I can't bear to think he will be going away without knowing."

"What news?" asked Daniel.

"He'll understand. I was planning to tell him, but I haven't found the right moment."

Daniel looked at Mary. He was in a hurry to get Darin's things to him before the train departed, but he saw moisture in Mary's eyes. He hesitated.

Daniel felt needed. He didn't know if he should comfort Mary or not. But she reached out and hugged him.

Daniel liked that Mary reached

to him for comfort. He returned the hug but let go before she did. Mary held on a minute longer.

Mary looked up at Daniel and their eyes fixed on each other. It was odd and they both felt peculiar. But Mary did not release the hug until a few seconds had passed.

"I'm sorry, Daniel," she said.

"I don't mind," he replied.

"You have to hurry," said Mary. "Let me know that he got off safely when you get back."

Daniel clutched the bag and tucked the note into his pocket. He turned and hurried out the door.

Mary cried as she pushed the door closed.

The train was about to depart when Daniel arrived. Darin had barely gotten his ticket. There were few people on the platform as the conductor had called for them to board. Steam rose from the engine.

Daniel scanned through the rail car windows searching for Darin.

There were a lot of people on board and he wasn't sure where Darin had boarded. Daniel hurried along the platform looking into each car. There! He saw him.

"Darin!" shouted Daniel.

The train started moving. The engine whistle blew.

Darin reached out the window to receive the bag, which Daniel handed off to him. Ever so slowly the train picked up speed. Little by little the wheels groaned. Keeping pace, Daniel reached in his pocket and pulled out Mary's note. He gave it to Darin. Darin looked puzzled.

"From your mother," he said.

"Thank you Daniel," shouted Darin.

"Headlines!" returned Daniel. "Headlines that sell papers!"

The train moved off in earnest and Daniel stopped jogging. He was out of breath.

Inside the railcar, Darin settled onto a wooden bench. The train was not overly crowded, but there were still a lot of people on board. Some held packages. Others settled back to read newspapers. A few just gazed ahead blankly.

Darin looked out the window as the train moved on down the tracks. New York City, he thought. A grand town it was.

Darin unfolded the letter.

Dear Son,

I will pray that God travels with you on your adventure to Cuba. Remember that He will protect you. I know you will do your job well and come back safe.

I did want to tell you that one of the reasons I came to visit is that I am planning to be married. I've met a wonderful man and he has asked me to marry him. He will never measure up to your father, but he is a good man and a good provider.

Hopefully I will see you when you get back and we can talk more about it then.

All my love,
Mom.

Darin smiled when he read the letter. It was great news. He had never met his father but he knew his mother was lonely without him. He read the letter a second time. It was good news indeed. His mother would be happy and that was important.

Darin settled back to enjoy the journey. It was exciting to be headed for Cuba. First he'd travel the eastern seaboard by train, then from Florida he'd take a boat and steam to Cuba. He'd see for himself what was going on and he'd write the best headlines in the world. He just knew he would.

Daniel was depressed. He should not have read Mary's note but on the trolley ride to the train station, curiosity got the better of him. It wasn't sealed. It was just folded. He was a newspaperman, a reporter. Curiosity was his strong point. He had only glanced at the note at first, but when he read that she was to be married he felt a kick in the gut.

He didn't understand his emotions. He liked Mrs. Connors. He liked her maybe too much. But she was his best friend's mother and it was strange to be attracted to her. There was a big age difference, but when he was with her, he didn't notice the age. She was youthful in her thoughts and so filled with life. And she looked to him for comfort. Daniel didn't know what to think of that. He enjoyed that she did that but he couldn't understand why he found himself thinking about her as much as he did.

The news that she was getting married should have been happy news, but it wasn't. Daniel felt almost betrayed. He fought away his thoughts. That was absurd. He barely knew this woman. But the few days she had been in New York were exciting and he relished the feeling of being around her. He couldn't help but feel a special connection to her.

The trolley ride home ended quickly. Daniel hardly noticed the trip and almost missed his stop when he arrived.

Daniel found himself walking home slowly. He could have taken a more direct route, but he didn't. New York City was a place filled with people, coming and going, hurrying this way or that. Yet, Daniel felt lonely.

A paperboy shouted the latest headline, *"McKinley Tells Spain To Stop Killing Rebels! Threatens Invasion!"*

Daniel smiled. That wasn't at all the real news. In fact, President McKinley wanted peace and had made it clear that a peaceful solution was in the best interest of both nations.

Daniel turned to read the name of the paper but couldn't see it because the boy moved on down the sidewalk. He knew it wasn't the *New York Empire*. At least they had some element of truth to their stories. He hoped.

Daniel trudged up the stairs toward Darin's apartment. He hesitated and then walked on by to his. He could talk to Mary later, he thought. It was getting toward the end of the day and he wanted a nap.

It was dark when Mary rapped on Daniel's door. He didn't expect a visitor and so he was startled out of his sleep. He was having an odd dream about a bunch of flowers. Tulips were growing everywhere. He got up and looked out the window. The city lights cast a strange hue on his bed.

"One moment," said Daniel.

"It's Mary," came the reply.

Daniel walked across the room and opened the door.

"Are you all right?" asked Mary softly.

"Yes. Come in."

Mary hesitated because the room was dark.

"Did Darin get on his way?"

"Yes, yes," said Daniel apologetically. "I'm sorry, I should have told you. I was tired and I just took a little nap."

"It's nine," said Mary.

"Oh," said Daniel. "Well I must have been more sleepy than I thought."

Mary felt uneasy.

"I'll go then."

"No," said Daniel. "Here, sit a minute."

Mary waited in the doorway and Daniel noticed her reluctance.

He reached over and lit the lamp.

"Sorry," said Daniel.

Mary came into the room and sat down.

"I'm worried about Darin," she said after a brief silence.

"He'll be fine," assured Daniel. He sat at the table across from her. "There's no real fighting where he's going."

"How can you be sure?"

"Well, truthfully," said Daniel slowly, "we can't. But it's not a revolt the way the papers say. All the stories are exaggerated. Even ours."

Mary forced out a little grin. She looked at Daniel.

"I, ah, I..." said Daniel.

"Mothers always worry--even about grown men."

The two looked at each other. A

clock on the wall ticked away loudly as the two gazed at each other without words.

"Mrs. Connors," said Daniel slowly. "I've enjoyed getting to know you."

"Me too," said Mary, "and you know I want you to call me Mary. Mrs. Connors sounds so old."

"You're not old."

Mary smiled. "Older than you."

"I don't feel like you're old."

"Old enough to be your mother," said Mary.

Daniel smiled. "That's not what I mean."

"What do you mean?"

"I mean, I've really enjoyed getting to know you. It's not like you're just my best friend's mom."

"And you are not just my son's best friend," said Mary.

Daniel slid his hand across the table toward Mary's hand.

"Mrs. Connors, I mean, Mary, you're a fascinating woman."

"Hmm," said Mary.

"I mean it. I know you're Darin's mother, but I feel attracted to you."

Mary didn't know what to say. She felt an attraction, too, but would have never said anything. She didn't understand her feelings. But she felt her heart beating strongly in her chest.

"I don't, I mean, I don't want to scare you. I just wanted you to know," said Daniel slowly.

"I find you to be intriguing, too," said Mary finally. "I don't know why, but from the first day I met you I've felt like I've known you. Oh, Darin has written me a lot of letters and he's talked about you. So I guess I do know you in a way. But this is..."

"Different," said Daniel interrupting.

"Different," said Mary slowly.

Daniel slid his hand to where he could touch Mary's. His finger barely rested on one of hers.

They peered into each others' souls. Daniel advanced his hand a tiny bit farther.

Without warning, Mary pulled

her hand away and stood up abruptly.

Daniel stood up too.

"I'm sorry," he said.

Mary did not speak, but stepped to the door and left.

Daniel looked at the closed door for a beat or two. "Well that was a mistake," he said aloud.

It was an hour or more later when Daniel heard a light tap on his door. He had made himself a late evening meal and was washing a dish at the sink.

With anticipation, he opened the door.

There, stood Mary. She was dressed in a simple blue dress, something she had made herself. Her hair had been combed and it shined.

Mary didn't speak at first and neither did Daniel.

Finally, quietly, Mary breathed a little sigh.

"Do you want to visit?"

Daniel pulled the door open a little wider.

"Yes, I would like that."

Mary walked slowly into the room as Daniel studied her.

"I mean, if you have the time," said Mary.

"Sure," said Daniel.

Daniel offered Mary a chair at the table. She walked past it and sat on a small couch in the corner of the room.

"You know I'm engaged to be married," she announced with shyness.

Daniel's mind jumped. He knew, but should he say?

"Oh?" he said finally. Daniel felt a lump in his throat.

"I came to visit Darin to tell him that."

"Congratulations," said Daniel slowly.

"Why do I feel you don't really mean that?" asked Mary.

"No, I do. Congratulations," said Daniel with a little more enthusiasm.

Mary smiled. "I can tell you're lying."

Daniel tilted his head to the side.

"I, he's a very lucky man," said

Daniel.

"Robert is a wonderful man," said Mary. She said the words, but her eyes undermined them.

Daniel pulled a chair up near the couch.

"I'm sure he will make you very happy," said Daniel.

"He will," said Mary.

"Do you think about him a lot?" asked Daniel.

Mary brushed her hair to the side. A tiny smile wandered onto her face. "No," she said. She knew Daniel was right. She thought about Darby more than Robert, and Daniel reminded her of Darby in some way. Since she met Daniel she found herself thinking about *him*, not Robert.

"Do you love him?" asked Daniel.

"Yes, I do."

"Now you're the one who's lying," said Daniel. "I hear hesitation in your voice."

"So this is how you reporters get the news?" said Mary quaintly.

"Sometimes." Daniel reached

out and grasped Mary's hand. She did not resist. Daniel felt his pulse quicken and he needed to drink something.

"So why marry someone if you are not sure about these things?"

Mary did not answer. She considered the question and her eyes gazed directly into Daniel's.

She reached over with her other hand and grasped Daniel's.

"Robert has been kind to me. He has helped me and he will be a good man for me."

"But there is no passion, is there?" asked Daniel.

"No," said Mary. "But that will grow."

Daniel leaned toward Mary. He gently tightened his grip on Mary's hand.

Mary felt her heart beating wildly.

Daniel licked his lips slightly.

"I want to kiss you," he said.

Mary did not respond.

Daniel leaned toward her and she did not move.

Slowly, Daniel got closer and closer until their lips met. It was a tiny kiss and ever so brief. Daniel put his hands on Mary's shoulders and then leaned back.

Mary reached up and touched the bottom of Daniel's chin and softly directed him closer. They kissed again. It wasn't long, but there was passion. They looked at each other silently when the kiss ended. Daniel moved to the couch with Mary and she leaned back against his chest. He held her. She felt safe. Without words they sat together in their embrace.

Time has an odd way of passing when you are sitting with someone to whom you are attracted. Mary thought about all kinds of things. Daniel thought about Mary. An hour passed, maybe two. Eventually Mary leaned toward Daniel to whisper.

"I better go."

"I'm glad you came by," said Daniel.

"Me, too."

Chapter 6

March 1898

New York, New York

The time Mary and Daniel spent together that evening changed things. Daniel had to work each day after that, but the evenings were spent out on the town with Mary or on long walks in Central Park. The park had originally been conceived in the 1850s as a place the wealthy could go to be seen, a sort of proof to European critics that New Yorkers were not without culture. The park cost $10 million to build and covered 840 acres. For many, it was paradise, green lawns and trees in stark contrast to the concrete maze of the city.

It reminded Mary of Scranton, Pennsylvania, and as she walked hand-in-hand with Daniel she often talked of girlhood memories in the hills around the coal mines. She hated the work and she hated her life at the mine, but she loved the plush green countryside of Pennsylvania.

She told Daniel about Darby. He asked, and she told him. She didn't mention Clarence Hillten, but rather, her time with a wonderful man who was so good to others, and who fought for them. She told Daniel she would always love Darby, that while she had only known him a short time, he was the kind of man you meet only once and you never forget, no matter what.

Daniel was a little bothered by her words because he had fallen in love with Mary and knew that he would probably never measure up to Darby. Mary, on the other hand, was confused, and she said so. She was planning to marry this Robert, but she was spending time with Daniel and she was doing it because she really liked him. She didn't know why exactly. He was young and funny and handsome and strong. What was there not to like? But they were of different generations, for sure, and while Mary allowed herself to kiss Daniel a few more times, she could feel herself holding back.

It was wrong, she thought. He'd ask and she would reply that she was confused. He'd back off and wonder.

"Word at the office," said Daniel, "is that Darin is on his way back. He should be here any day."

"I'm so glad," said Mary. She was indeed relieved because she had worried about Darin since he left.

"The managing editor said he did a terrific job and they are talking about giving him a raise."

"That's wonderful," said Mary.

"Your son is really a good worker," said Daniel.

Mary stopped and pulled Daniel to a park bench.

"You know, Daniel," she said softly, "I'm really fond of you. And these last few weeks have been wonderful. You're such a romantic man and every woman loves that."

"But?" interrupted Daniel.

"I guess you knew there was a 'but' coming?"

"Yes," said Daniel. "I'm a newspaper reporter, remember?"

Mary looked out across a small pond and watched some Mallard ducks glide slowly toward the other side.

"But," she said with a sigh, "this is not something my son is going to accept."

"What?" asked Daniel a little surprised. "You and me? Darin will be happy for us."

"No," said Mary, "he won't. I'm his mother. You're his friend. You're the same age as him. He's not going to understand."

Daniel reached for one of Mary's hands.

"What's going on between us?" he asked curtly. He couldn't help it. He loved her and he wanted to know where he stood.

"I don't know," said Mary quietly. "I don't know what this is. I don't think it's right."

"What, that two people are attracted to each other? You know I love you," said Daniel.

"I know you do," said Mary.

"Do you love me?" asked Daniel.

Mary looked at him. "I don't know, Daniel. I love being with you. You make me laugh so much, and you make me feel so young! But look at us. We're so different."

"Different? We're not all that different. We both want the same thing in life. We just want to be happy, to be with someone who cares for us." He paused. "Is it the age?"

"Well, look at us," protested Mary.

"Look at what? I see you and I see a beautiful woman, a woman who is kind and gentle..." said Daniel.

"And a woman who has a son your exact age," finished Mary.

"I don't care about that. I don't see age when I'm with you. All I see is you. I just want to be with you. It doesn't matter about anything in the past or or how old you are or how old I am. Age is just a number."

Mary smiled. "You flatter me."

"Don't marry Robert," said Daniel.

Mary looked away slowly. She didn't know what to say. She thought about Robert. Robert was a good man. Robert had been kind to her and had helped her through rough days and Robert was her own age.

"Robert," said Mary. She didn't finish her sentence.

"You don't love Robert the way I love you," said Daniel.

Mary looked back at Daniel. "Why are you making this hard for me?"

Daniel hugged her. "I don't mean to make it hard. I just want you to know that I'm here and I will be good to you and I will take care of you and I will love you."

"I know you will," said Mary.

The two left the park and walked back toward the apartment building. For awhile Daniel held Mary's hand, but at times she wiggled it loose and did not return to holding his hand.

Daniel felt as though he was losing her. He could not understand why she liked him so much, but wouldn't let the relationship grow. What was holding her back? Darin would be home soon and Daniel thought that that would signal the end.

"A penny for your thoughts," said Mary finally.

Daniel looked at Mary as they walked. He bit his lip.

"Are you going back soon?"

"Yes," said Mary. "A few days after Darin returns I need to head back. I've already been here a month."

They neared the apartment building and so Daniel stopped suddenly and slowly pushed Mary against the wall of the building. He kissed her. She responded. It was a deep kiss and it lasted.

"We can't," said Mary.

"We can't what?" asked Daniel.

"I'm engaged to be married."

Daniel kissed her again. Mary

felt a warmth come over her. She gasped for air briefly.

"I want you," said Daniel.

"I want you, too," returned Mary.

"Then forget about what's his name." Daniel kissed Mary hard.

"Oh, God," she said. "What are we doing?"

"Acting like adults," said Daniel. He took her hand and pulled her into the apartment building and up the stairs. It had become twilight outside and the stairwell was dark.

Up to the apartment Daniel led her. She felt like a young girl. Part of her said, "no," but most of her said "yes."

Daniel fumbled with the keys and then swung open the door. Mary followed. With the lights off, they kissed again. Daniel held Mary's wrists with each of his hands. He backed her toward his bed as they kissed.

Mary's legs bumped against the bed. She wanted him to stop, but she tugged him and they fell backwards into the bed.

"I want you so much," Mary whispered with a deeper voice.

Daniel reached down and pushed up her skirt. She took a long, deep breath as he caressed her thigh. One hand continued to hold her wrist while the other exposed her undergarment. He glanced to see it was black. Mary used her free hand to tug Daniel toward her and they kissed.

Daniel was pretty rough on her, but she liked it, and their lovemaking was a little wild. Others in the apartment might have heard the passion--but they didn't care.

Morning came early. Daniel did not want to leave the arms of Mrs. Connors but he had to get to work. In the morning light, Daniel noticed her smiling at him. He kissed her and went off to the newspaper office.

Mary's head was filled with contradiction. She loved what they did, but she was plagued with guilt. It just didn't seem right. She dressed and resigned herself to spend the day getting ready to leave for California. Just as soon as Darin returned home she'd leave. That was her decision.

Darin got off the train the next day. His skin was darker from all the time spent in the sun. He looked worn out from the travel. His mother met him at the station and as he collected his bag, he remembered the news.

"Oh, so you're getting married?"

"Yes," said Mary.

"Anybody I know?" asked Darin.

"No, I met Robert sometime after you left home. He's different from your father, but he's a good man."

"The important thing is," said Darin, "will you be happy?"

"I'll be happy," Mary said. It was the pat answer. She had long since convinced herself that Robert would make her happy. But deep inside, now that there was Daniel, she wasn't sure.

Darin stopped walking at the trolley depot. He put his bag down.

"How's Daniel?" he asked softly.

Mary's mind panicked.

She said the first thing that came to her mind.

"Daniel?"

"Yes, Daniel," said Darin. He thought her answer was odd. "How's Daniel?"

"He's fine," said Mary, hoping her response did not give away her true feelings.

"Has he shown you around New York?"

"Yes," said Mary. "He's been a terrific host."

"He's a good lad," said Darin.

The trolley arrived and they boarded.

Darin was glad to get home. It was all neat and looked radically better. He was so tired he crashed on the divan without making it into its bed. Mary sat in the corner of the room watching him. Her son had grown up to be a man. She was proud of him.

Mary made herself busy by straightening up the apartment she had already organized.

Her thoughts were random. She'd think about Darby, and then Clarence Hillten, then Robert, then Daniel. She compared Daniel to Darby. There were similarities. She couldn't help but feel that. But Robert was nothing like Clarence Hillten. Robert was successful and he was kind to his people. He was always more than kind to her. But Daniel was exciting. That was Daniel to a tee. He had energy and life and spirit and he was fun. Robert could be fun. But Robert was not as much fun. Yet Daniel was just a boy. He didn't act like a boy, but he was so young. He was so very young.

Mary just did not know what to do. She sighed. Why couldn't there be a simple answer? Youth and passion on the one hand, she thought, seniority and stability on the other. She wanted both, but she could not have both. Should she leave for home and do what she had promised to do, or should she stay and follow a dream?

Darin slept straight through the

night. Mary had to use his spot in the closet. It wasn't comfortable. She tossed and turned most of the night. She opened her eyes to complete darkness and had an odd thought. Would this be what it would be like to be dead?

When morning finally came, Mary was up early.

Daniel came by while she was making coffee. He was on his way to work but wanted to see how Darin was doing and to speak to Mary.

Mary greeted him at the door with a long hug. Daniel kissed her lightly.

"What the hell?" asked Darin suddenly.

Daniel responded by stepping back. Mary touched her mouth.

"What are you doing?" asked Darin with anger in his voice.

"How are you doing?" asked Daniel, trying to change the subject.

Darin leaned up from the divan. "What the hell did I just see?"

Mary turned to him with a lost look on her face.

"Did you kiss my mother?" asked Darin pointedly.

"Look, Darin," said Daniel.

"No, don't 'look' me. Did you just kiss my mother on the lips?"

"Darin," said Mary.

"You stay out of this," ordered Darin as he pointed at her.

"Listen," said Daniel.

"Just give me a 'yes' or 'no' answer."

"I love your mother," said Daniel. Mary hurried over to the kitchen.

"Oh, God!" said Darin. "I can't believe this." Darin pointed in Mary's direction. "That's my mother!"

"Yes, and so what? I love her! What's so wrong with that?"

"You love her?" Darin said with amazement. "You love my mother? You kissed my mother? This is my MOTHER." His anger grew. Darin stepped to the door and started pushing it shut. "You just get the hell out of here."

"Darin," said Daniel. Darin shut the door. He stared at it and then turned to Mary.

"What were you thinking?"

Mary turned toward the counter and stirred her coffee.

"What? Is everybody crazy here? I leave for a few days and my best friend falls in love with my mother? I think I'm going to be sick." Darin went into the bathroom.

Quietly, Mary tilted her head down and tears flowed out of her eyes. "I'm sorry," she said. Darin did not hear. "I'm so sorry."

Mary boarded the train for home two days later. Darin hardly spoke to her while preparing for the trip and he forbade Daniel to go with them to see her off. At the station, the only cause for talk was to announce the train was about to leave.

After checking the trunk, Darin placed Mary's light luggage on board, next to her seat.

"I love you, son," said Mary. Darin looked at her but did not answer. She reached out to hug him but he pulled away. "I love you, Darin."

"Goodbye, Mother," was all Darin said.

The trip back toward Los Angeles was agonizing. Mary hated herself for what she had done. She wished that she had restrained herself. She wished that she had just married Robert and never gone to New York. The outcome was the same in the end, she would marry Robert anyway, except, her heart was broken. How, she thought, could one woman's life be so miserable?

Riding the train by oneself is lonely enough, but riding it broken-hearted was torture.

It was nighttime somewhere in Nebraska when Mary discovered a folded note stuck in her bag. She opened it. Tears dropped on the letter as she read it. Some of the ink ran. It was from Daniel.

Dear, Dear Mary,

Please don't go back to Califor-

nia. I do love you. I know this is all so unusual. But I don't want you to go. Maybe you feel the answer is there, but it's not. You and I are meant to be together. Please don't go. I don't want you to go.

Daniel

Mary held the letter and wept. What was she going to do? Why wasn't there an answer?

Chapter 7

October 31, 2008

San Antonio, Texas

It was Halloween and the nurses had set up a couple of paper pumpkins and a skeleton or two at the nurses' station. Running an ICU was tough work and even the nurses needed a little festivity from time-to-time to get through the day.

The ethics committee was reviewing Lauri's case. She was in a coma, 7T, doing better, but no one had found any next-of-kin. The county was paying the tab and the hospital administrator had asked that somebody be located to see if there was insurance or any other kind of support.

A constable dropped by to report that the driver's license details had not produced any leads. He had even been by the address and determined that she evidently lived alone. On the back of the license it said she was willing to be an organ donor in the event of death.

Wallace was improving, but still in a wheel chair. There was talk by the doctors of his release, "in a few days," they told him. His trips to see Lauri were routine and as he was wheeled past the nurses' station, the staff called him by name.

Inside Lauri's area, Wallace always reached over and held her hand. Her hands had become customary to him. It was strange that they were limp but warm. Wallace had studied Lauri's hands intently. He wondered about her. Who was she, really? How did they come to be in such a predicament, and where did she come from?

Wallace thought about his suicide attempt. That would have been totally stupid, he reasoned. It would not have solved anything.

But how was it that Lauri happened along? Why did she get a flat on her car--then, and there? Why that time and place? Of all the things that happen on a daily basis, why that? And there was that feeling of intense connection. What was that?

He had studied a lot of different things in graduate school. Psychology was an advanced science. But nobody had ever much addressed the idea of past lives. No, actually, they had never addressed it at all. It just wasn't discussed. Stuff like that was *parapsychology,* outside the realm of the study of psychology.

Wallace looked at Lauri's face. The lacerations had improved and there were fewer bandages. She was bruised and banged up. But other than that, she looked just like she was sleeping. The ventilator made a rhythmic noise. One of the nurses had said that they were weaning her off the machine, that she had breathed without it several times for fifteen minute trials.

"Lauri," said Wallace finally,

"I'm here. I know you can hear me. You know you are going to be all right. You know you are going to come out of this thing."

Wallace moved his head closer to Lauri's.

"We met for a reason. You need to wake up so that we can figure out what that is."

A nurse hurried into the area.

"Hello Mr. Larame. How's she doing?"

"I was about to ask you. She looks the same," said Wallace.

The nurse checked the equipment.

"Everything looks good."

The nurse adjusted the sheet that was covering Lauri and moved her legs into a different position. She turned her body onto its side and moved her pillow.

Just watching that depressed Wallace. Lauri was alive but her being was missing. She was inside there somewhere, but for days she did not respond or give any indication that she was coming out of it. They had been feeding her with a tube.

Wallace had been told by one of his nurses that the ethics committee was looking at her case. He didn't understand why. She had improved. Her coma had lessened. Surely they would never consider unplugging any of the equipment that was keeping her alive. They only do that when the brain dies, and her brain was far from dead.

Wallace squeezed Lauri's hand. He was frustrated, and angry.

"Lauri, wake up. This is Wallace. I'm here with you. I need you to talk to me. I need you to open your eyes and look at me. I know you can hear me." He felt a little twinge of pain in his liver where the surgeon had stitched him back together.

Richard Strain walked up behind Wallace.

"You know that really works."

"What?" asked Wallace.

"Studies show that comatose patients benefit a great deal from hearing people talk to them while they are in a coma."

Wallace looked at him. "Aren't you the organ recovery guy? Why are you here?" Wallace's voice was agitated.

"Yes, I am. But don't worry. We're not taking anybody's organs. She's improved since I first saw her, was better yesterday and the neurologist says she is better still today."

"So why *are* you here?"

"I just came to see her, that's all," said Richard. "I was here in the hospital meeting with a family whose son was in a severe motorcycle accident. No helmet."

"He dead?" asked Wallace.

"He's a 3 on the Glasgow coma scale."

"So he's brain dead?"

"I'm afraid so."

"So you're not here for Lauri?" said Wallace.

"Not at all. I just came to see how she was doing. I was on the floor and just had the urge to see her. She is not out of the woods yet, but she has a good chance of full recovery. When they come in as a 5T and improve to a 7T that's a good sign. That's a very good sign."

"I thought you were here for her organs," said Wallace.

"I'm really sorry," said Richard, "sometimes people look at me like the grim reaper." He put his hand on Lauri's shoulder. "But this young lady is going to be using her organs. Hopefully for a long time to come."

"God, your job must be hard," said Wallace.

"Yeah," said Richard, "but you'd be surprised how satisfying it is to turn a tragedy into a miracle. That young boy who just died will save the lives of four other people."

"How?" asked Wallace.

"Two kidneys, a liver and a heart for certain. His corneas will probably go to help someone, depending if they can be salvaged after the accident. It's actually very satisfying to know that his tragic sacrifice will allow others to live longer lives."

"I see," said Wallace. "I just didn't want..."

"No," said Richard. "She's going in the right direction. She's got a lot of life ahead of her."

Richard shook Wallace's hand, touched Lauri on the forehead and looked at her for a moment.

"There's something about this woman," said Richard. He shook his head ever so slightly from side to side. "She'll be all right." Then, as quickly as he had appeared, he walked out.

Wallace was relieved. He was afraid some bureaucratic maneuver was in play to unplug her and cut her up. Wallace leaned his head on his hand. He felt bad. His pain killers were wearing off and he could feel the injuries inside.

"Lauri," he said. "I'm going to go. But I'll be back later today. We're going to get you through this."

It was time, and one of the aides came to retrieve Wallace in his wheelchair.

Hospitals are no place to get well. Wallace was restless and bored. It took awhile to get another round of pain killers and that irritated Wallace. Rules. He hated them.

Wallace's bout of self-pity ended abruptly when one of the aides rushed in.

"She's awake, Mr. Larame! Breathing on her own! The endotracheal tube is out!"

"What?" asked Wallace.

"Doctor said to bring you over."

"Lauri's awake?"

"Yes, yes, c'mon."

Wallace rolled out of bed into the wheelchair and the lady pushed him down the hall double time. Several people stepped out of the way as the team zoomed past. A couple of nurses looked up from their work and one doctor did a little dance to make way.

In the ICU there was a crowd of personnel. The neurologist examined Lauri, looked into her eyes with his light.

"Thirsty," said Lauri in a hoarse

voice.

Someone handed her a tiny cup of ice chips.

"Well thank God," said Dr. Rigdon, finally. "This is great."

Wallace's chair was pushed closer to the bed. Lauri saw him and instantly reached for him. Her arm was still restrained. Wallace leaned up out of his chair and hugged her. The cup of ice spilled and three nurses scrambled to clean it up.

Fields fought back tears as she watched the scene from a distance.

"What happened?" whispered Lauri in Wallace's ear.

Wallace breathed.

"I'm so glad to see you," he said.

"What's going on?" asked Lauri.

"You were in a car accident," answered Dr. Rigdon. "You've just come out of a coma."

Wallace released his grip so that he could look into Lauri's eyes. She looked back. There was a crowd of people around but she was unaware of them. Their eyes made a connection no one else could understand.

"I dreamed weird stuff, and I dreamed you were here."

"I was," said Wallace.

"What happened?"

"I'm sorry. I'm so sorry."

"We were in a wreck?"

"Yeah, just as soon as we left the cemetery."

Lauri managed a small smile. "I can see the headlines on that one, '*Couple Survives Car Wreck At Cemetery*'."

Wallace smiled. He sat back into his wheelchair but held on to Lauri's hand.

"I'm so glad you're back."

"You were here with me?" asked Lauri.

"Right here."

"I heard your voice."

"I'm glad."

"Tell her 'no'," said Lauri.

"What?" asked Wallace.

Lauri closed her eyes.

"What did you say?"

"I don't know," said Lauri softly.

Dr. Rigdon put his hand on

Lauri's face and felt of it. He pinched her arm.

"Oweo," she said as she pulled away.

"Very good," said the doctor.

"What the hell?" responded Lauri.

"Do you know what season it is?" asked Dr. Rigdon.

Lauri looked puzzled. "Um, fall?" she asked.

"What month?"

"October."

"Good."

The doctor placed his stethoscope on Lauri's chest.

"She's breathing well."

"I have to pee," said Lauri as she opened her eyes.

"That's okay," said the doctor. "Just go ahead."

"Nooo," protested Lauri as her eyes darted to see the people in the area.

"Go ahead and relieve yourself," said Dr. Rigdon. "You have a foley catheter."

"What?"

"We inserted a tube. It's okay to relieve yourself."

Lauri pushed her bladder. She gently bit her own lip as she did.

Dr. Rigdon waved his hand to get the group to give more space.

Wallace squeezed Lauri's hand lightly.

Finally, Lauri smiled a little.

"Well, that's embarrassing," she said.

The nurses approved. That step was important.

Lauri looked around at all the people.

"What is this, the national nurses' convention?"

The ladies laughed.

"Welcome back, honey," said one of the staff.

Dr. Rigdon stood back and looked at the patient.

"Let's see if she can eat a little bit *per os* later today," said the doctor. He spoke a little louder. "Do you want to try to eat something? Are you hungry?"

Wallace smiled. What's up with doctors, he thought. Why do they talk louder to patients? They're not hearing impaired. Wallace squeezed Lauri's hand and she looked at him. She smiled back at Wallace and drew strength from his eyes.

Lauri didn't answer the question the doctor asked. It didn't matter. He hadn't waited for an answer. He was suddenly off giving instructions to the nurses and like so many doctors, disappeared behind the curtains.

Richard Strain had heard the news and he reappeared about the time the nursing staff evaporated off to their chores.

"Well look at this," he said in a jovial voice. He made imaginary quotes in the air when he spoke. *"Another one comes back from never-never land."*

Lauri looked at Wallace with a 'who's this?' look on her face. She saw those hand motions and had a weird feeling inside.

"It's a great day to be awake, isn't it?" he asked.

Lauri nodded her head slightly.

Wallace pulled himself closer to the bed.

"Well you are a miracle woman," said Richard. "You came in a 5T and now the doctor has you right up there close to the top. Thirteen, maybe 14. Yesterday they tried you without the ventilator, today you don't need it at all."

"What?" asked Lauri as she looked at Wallace.

"Oh," said Richard a little apologetically, "on the coma scale. You came into the hospital with a pretty severe brain injury. The swelling caused you to drop into a coma and you were rated 5T. That's not good. But you fought it back, you came up to a 7T right away and now you're pushing 14.

"It means, young lady, that you are going to recover and walk out of here with one heck of a story."

"Fourteen?"

"Fifteen is the max. Everyone working here is a 15. You're almost back. You don't know what a big step that is. Medication worked to shrink the swelling, this man here held your hand and talked you through it, you're a miracle."

Lauri smiled. "P-r-a-i-s-e Je--sus," she said in a joking voice.

Richard laughed. "I love it when people live," he said.

"Yeah, me too," she said, still hoarse.

Richard looked at her silently.

"You seem familiar. Have you been in the hospital before?"

"No," she said. "Nothing like this."

"I'm Richard Strain. I just feel like I've seen you around."

"Don't know," she said.

"Well, no worries. I'm just so pleased you are back among the living. Another one of God's miracles."

"So she's going to be okay?" asked Wallace.

"Absolutely. It will take a little while to get back to normal, but this young lady is a fighter. She'll sleep a lot at first, but that's good. The body needs to repair that ol' noggin. Just remember how lucky you are. God's given you a gift."

"Thank you doctor," said Lauri.

"Oh, I'm not a doctor," said Richard. "I'm an RN. I've taught a few doctors how to transplant organs, but no, you can leave that doctor business up to the guys in the long white coats."

"You do transplants?" asked Wallace.

"Used to do them. I consult now and I help out. Used to fly in with the heart in an ice chest. You've never seen anything so amazing as when you hook that heart up in a new body and it starts beating. Sends chills down my back every time."

Lauri's eyes were closed and she drifted to sleep.

Wallace thanked Richard. Eventually the staff wheeled him away. He had forgotten about his own pain. Seeing Lauri with her eyes open was indeed a moment of joy.

Wallace was discharged from the

hospital first. A week later Lauri was released. Wallace had been to see her every day and she had agreed to come live with him at least until she had returned to full health. He didn't want her living by herself and he had a big empty house where she could have the guest room.

Wallace actually ran his practice out of his home, but he had stopped seeing patients. He was fed up with the business and he felt totally inept at helping them. His study was filled with books, floor to ceiling, and he had a large antique couch with ornate wood where the clients could recline and talk about their darkest troubles. Wallace had grown to hate the work. The psychiatrists loaded their patients up with drugs and to his way of thinking, caused more problems than they fixed. As a psychologist, he didn't believe in psychotropic medication, couldn't prescribe it anyway, hated the side effects.

His business was based upon his ability to talk, to get people to understand how they can better deal with their lives, to give them new ways to cope.

But that wasn't all that effective either, because the same patients kept coming back. That's probably why he had fallen into despair. He liked his patients, but nobody ever got cured. They told him they appreciated him, they said they couldn't go on without him, but then, the second some shrink came along and offered them meds, a lot of them jumped at the chance.

Wallace knew the dangers of that, had seen it many times. All you have to do is read the package inserts or the Physician's Desk Reference, scan down the list of associated side effects and the only thing you'll wind up taking without fear is aspirin.

Wallace was glad Lauri was there. She was so sweet and they talked for hours about every imaginable subject.

She did say she was having some strange thoughts since the accident, things she had never experienced before. She had vivid dreams and odd visions of people, words, faces. She didn't understand it and it bothered her. She wanted to know where all that was coming from. She felt things. She sensed movement in the house, heard noises, looked around from time to time, got chills.

Wallace listened carefully to her and realized that something unusual had happened to her. He wasn't sure what. But he believed her. She even seemed to read his thoughts sometimes. Not a lot, but she would speak when he started to speak and they'd laugh and realize they were about to say the same thing.

And then there were those visions of the past. Those were strange. They both somehow knew things about people in the past that they could not possibly know and what was even more weird was that they had exactly the same memories. It was as if they did know each other in previous lives, a lot of lives. They had lived and died, *together*, many times.

There was plenty of material on the internet about reincarnation but Wallace could not find a single case where two people had identical memories of multiple lives. It was logical. If past existences were real, and he was convinced that they were, how was it that they kept meeting up? Was it the pact between Meallan and Dubhghall? Was that it? *Look for me. I will find you.*

Wallace had not hypnotized anyone in a long time so his confidence was a little shaken before Lauri leaned back on his couch for an attempt.

Lauri was a willing subject and that was good. He made sure she was comfortable and asked her to hold up her hand and concentrate on it. She giggled a little.

"It's not going to work if you don't believe," said Wallace.

"Okay, okay, I believe," she said.

Wallace asked her to concentrate on the middle finger as she moved her hand closer and closer to her face, ever so slowly.

As her eyes stayed on her finger, they felt a little heavy. Wallace was pleased. He talked her into a state of peace and restfulness. He used a soft monotone, and told her to imagine floating on a cloud.

In just a few minutes, her eyes closed. Wallace snapped his fingers and told her she was asleep, but that she could hear everything he was saying.

He told her to put her hand down.

Wallace nodded his head with approval when she did.

The unconscious state, he thought, 'amazing'. Fully alert, but in a trance. Not everyone is susceptible. But Lauri seemed like she had a high suggestibility index and it sure appeared that way.

He asked her to lean forward. She did. He asked her to turn her head from side-to-side. She did.

"Lauri," he said, "I know you can hear me. I want you to look into your mind and see if you can remember Meallan. See if you can picture a young girl meeting with a young man, on the side of a river. It's a nice night. Can you see that?"

"Yes," she said. "Yes, I feel it. It smells so fresh. The river is running. But it's tense. It's scary. Everyone is scared. There are a lot of people really scared."

"Can you see those people?"

"No," she said. "Well, yes, I see them walking. They're carrying things. They're tired. And they are afraid. I feel a lot of fear."

"Are you afraid?"

"Yes!" she said loudly.

"It's okay. It's fine," said Wallace. "Nothing is going to hurt you."

"I'm so scared," said Lauri, almost like a little girl.

"Do you see Dub?"

Lauri did not respond.

"Do you see a soldier?"

"Dub?"

Wallace leaned toward Lauri.

"Is Dub there?"

"Yes," she said. "I love you."

"You love Dub?"

"I do love you. Don't go. Don't fight. Something bad is going to happen to you. It's terrible. I know it. Don't go, Dub. You have to jump to the left. Watch it!" Lauri started crying.

Wallace listened for a minute.

"What's happening now?"

"Don't do it," she said. "It's a mistake. He doesn't love you."

"Who doesn't?"

"I don't know. He just doesn't," said Lauri softly.

"Is it Dub?"

"No!" Lauri said abruptly.

"No! You can't! You can't!" Lauri was keenly agitated.

"You're okay. You're fine."

Lauri breathed heavily. Her chest rose and fell. She licked her lips. Her fingers clenched.

"What's happening now?" asked Wallace.

"Oh, God yes. Oh God. Oh God."

Wallace observed closely. Lauri settled down.

"Lauri, I am going to bring you out of your sleep, now. When I snap my fingers you are going to open your eyes and you are going to remember everything you just heard, or saw, or felt."

Wallace snapped his fingers.

Lauri opened her eyes suddenly.

"That was weird," she said.

"Welcome to the world of hypnosis."

"Wow. That's very strange. I feel aroused a little."

"That's okay. That can happen."

"No really. I mean, really." Lauri squirmed a little to readjust her position on the recliner. "That hasn't happened in a long time."

"Do you have any idea what just happened?"

"You mean? No, not really. I went back?"

"Hypnotic regression. You just went back into a past existence. Those things you and I have been feeling. They're in your mind. We brought it back."

"But what does that mean? Is it

real or is it imagination?"

"I don't know," said Wallace. "Maybe it is real, maybe it isn't."

"How could that be?" asked Lauri. "You and I have the same thoughts."

"That is pretty remarkable," said Wallace slowly.

"Have we lived past lives together?"

"Could be," said Wallace. "Could be you have those thoughts and you have implanted them in my mind."

"Oh, bull," said Lauri. "How would I do that?"

"Telepathy?"

"No way," said Lauri. "We both felt the same things. We know. Don't you remember, in the cemetery? We knew each other before. I knew *you* before."

"I know," said Wallace. "I'm just saying."

"Saying what?"

"I'm just looking at the other possibilities. Nobody is going to believe us. Nobody is going to believe that two souls came together and they both had the same memory of past lives together. Nobody has ever reported that before."

"So why can't it be that this is the first time?"

"It could be."

"The pact. It's because of the pact. *Look for me...*" Lauri hesitated for the response.

"*I will find you,*" answered Wallace.

"How can that be telepathy?" asked Lauri.

"I don't know. I don't think it is telepathy. I think what we are feeling is real."

"Just that you don't really believe it," challenged Lauri.

"I don't know what I believe. How am I supposed to know about something like this?"

"Don't you feel it?" asked Lauri.

"I do feel it. That's just it. I do feel it. I've never felt anything like this before."

"Okay, so go with the feeling," concluded Lauri.

"Yes, but, how do we prove this? How do we convince others?"

"We don't have to convince others. We feel what we feel. We *know* what we know."

"Maybe you're right," said Wallace. "Maybe that's all that matters."

"That *is* all that matters. Why should we care what people think?" asked Lauri.

Wallace got up from his seat and sat down on the recliner beside Lauri. He lifted up one of her hands.

"It's just strange," he said. "Why do I know you so well?"

"I guess it is because we've known each other for so long. How many hundreds of years have we been together?"

"Do you hear how crazy that sounds?" asked Wallace.

"I don't care. I knew you before. I knew you before."

Wallace leaned down and kissed Lauri on the forehead.

Chapter 8

April 4, 1898

Los Angeles, California

Mary was not excited. On the contrary, she felt trapped. She had returned to California and did everything possible to put Daniel out of her mind.

A couple of telegrams came but she did not open them. She knew what they would say and could not bear to read what she knew Daniel was feeling.

It would make no sense for her to go back to New York. Robert was a good man and he had courted her properly. He had asked her to marry him and she had told him "yes."

But every single day leading up

to the wedding, she questioned herself. Her heart did not belong with Robert. That much she knew. Her mind was with Robert. Marrying him was the logical thing to do. But she didn't want to listen to her mind. She wanted to listen to her heart.

She cried a lot before the wedding and Robert wanted to know why. He didn't comfort her the way she needed to be comforted. She just needed to be held, not interrogated.

On the morning of the wedding, Mary threw up. Her friend Elizabeth, told her it was just nerves.

"You'll be all right, honey," said Elizabeth. "You're just nervous about all this. Everyone feels this way." Elizabeth was a little older than Mary, and chubby and short. But she was very sweet and loving and she had known Mary for a long time.

"I can't do this," said Mary. "I can't go through with this. It's a mistake. He doesn't love me."

"Honey, I felt the same way before I married Rufus. It's natural."

"There's nothing natural about throwing up," said Mary. "This is the most unnatural thing I can think about doing, now or any other time."

Elizabeth offered Mary a towel. Mary wiped her mouth.

"I feel so sick," said Mary.

"It'll pass," said Elizabeth in her southern drawl.

"Oh, God," said Mary. "It's not supposed to feel so wrong."

"You'll get over it," said Elizabeth.

Mary sat up straight on the side of her bed.

"I love you, Elizabeth, but is there any possible way you can stop saying that?" she asked sharply.

"There, there," she said as she patted Mary on the shoulders.

"Uah. I feel so light-headed."

"Hmm, huh," agreed Elizabeth, not wanting to say anything that would offend her friend.

Outside the bedroom where Mary was getting ready, guests arrived for the wedding in the courtyard.

Robert was a muckety-muck at the bank where he worked and his friends came from high society. Mary peered out the window and then closed the lace curtains tightly. She had not seen Robert and, for some reason, she did not want to see him now.

The thought of marrying Robert was growing more and more repulsive. She could not get Daniel's image out of her mind and she could not stop thinking about what they had done in his apartment. He made her feel so free and so alive. His touch was both gentle and commanding.

Mary reached for the basin again and hung her head. Elizabeth patted her back. Mary gagged a little but did not throw up.

"It makes no sense," said Mary.

"What's that, honey?" asked Elizabeth.

"Why does God do this?"

"Do what?"

"I've already thrown up and there is nothing left to throw up. So why does he keep making me gag?"

"Now, now," said Elizabeth.

Mary looked up at Elizabeth. There were tears in her eyes from straining. Her nose was runny. She felt awful and thought to herself that she probably looked worse.

"Thank you, Elizabeth. You're a real friend."

Elizabeth managed a tiny smile. "You're welcome, honey."

The wedding was due to get underway at 1 o'clock sharp. That's what the expensive invitations said and by that time all the seats were filled. Mary wasn't ready. She was on her feet and Elizabeth and two other girls helped her put on her dress and they fixed her face.

She was beautiful, but she was not glowing. Inside, she just wanted to run. Her marrying Robert was the envy of a number of women in the audience. But she didn't care and didn't want to do it. Her mind was dizzy with confusion.

The best man from the wedding party stuck his head in for the third time to determine the source of the delay.

Mary looked at him and abruptly peeled off her veil.

"I can't do this," she said. "No, I can't. I can't."

The ladies looked at her with mouths open.

"What?" asked the best man.

"Tell Robert, I can't do this," said Mary.

Elizabeth hurried over to the best man.

"She's a little nervous. She'll be all right," she whispered.

"I will not be all right," said Mary where everyone could hear. "Tell Robert to come in here."

"What are you saying?" asked the best man.

"You heard me," said Mary.

"Perhaps I did," said the best man, "but I'm having a little trouble believing what you said."

"Oh, darn you!" said Mary. "Can

you please tell Robert that I want to talk to him?"

The best man hurried out of the room. The ladies attempted to continue preparing Mary, but she brushed them away and sat soundly on the bed. An expensive fuel lamp shook and one of the women grabbed it to stabilize it.

Through the window it was possible to see the best man approach Robert, whose back was to the window. Arms flailed and there was consternation. Mary watched a moment and then stood up and bolted out the back door. She made some demands to a gentleman standing beside a motorcar and before Robert knew what hit, Mary was gone.

Mary did not look back. She thought about Darby and Daniel and she made her mind up that she was not ever going to marry Robert. It was a huge scandal, and Mary knew it would be, but she didn't care. Something in her told her to follow her heart.

Mary boarded the train for New York the following morning. Before she left, Robert sent two different people to her place to speak with her but she refused to see them. Odd, she thought, that Robert didn't bother to come himself. Gutless, she thought, he was probably just trying to save face for his high society crowd.

But it was all behind her now. The train chugged up the long steep grade as steam bellowed from the engine.

Mary felt driven, somehow. She'd left a complete life behind, with the potential of living well with a well-connected man. Yet, even though she had told him she did, she knew she really didn't love him. It was an act. It was the act of a single older woman, giving in to the pressures of society. "Where's the Mister?" people would ask. She hated it. The love of her life was Darby and he was gone and marrying Robert would have just been to please people.

Daniel, though, Daniel, he was

very interesting. Way too young, of course--he was her son's friend! But there was something about Daniel that enthralled Mary. She felt passion for him. She felt something she had never felt for Robert. She felt about him the way she had once felt about Darby.

Chapter 9

April 10, 1898

New York, New York

Mary had not wired Daniel and he was stunned when he opened the door to his apartment to see her standing there. She was exhausted from her trip and tired from hauling her bag up the stairs in Daniel's building.

Daniel looked at her, and she at him, until Daniel reached out and hugged her.

"Mary!" he said with assertion. "It's good to see you," he said a little more softly.

"I'm sorry, Daniel," said Mary.

"Nonsense," replied Daniel.

"I should have sent a telegram."

"No, this is a great surprise. Come in, please."

Daniel scooped up Mary's belongings and ushered her into his apartment. Mary grabbed him and kissed him. Daniel returned the kiss without closing the door to his room.

"What made you change your mind?" asked Daniel softly.

"I just couldn't do it," she said. "I couldn't marry Robert when all I was doing was thinking about you every five minutes."

Daniel squeezed her.

"But what about Robert now?"

"I don't want you to feel bad about it," she said. "I don't want your heart to hurt. I love you more than I thought. I don't ever want you to feel sad, especially not because of me."

"As long as you're not hurt," said Daniel.

"I couldn't stay there. I had to come to you."

Daniel felt flush. He didn't understand, but it felt right to him.

"I so love you," he said.

Mary leaned back from their embrace and looked at Daniel. Tears streamed down her face.

"I'm so in love with you," she whispered as she gazed directly into his eyes. "Something told me to come to you. Something said I should do this."

Slowly, Daniel kissed her again. "I'm glad you're here with me," he breathed.

Then, without notice, Darin burst into the room. "What are you doing?" he demanded. "Damn it, Mother!"

Darin shoved Daniel back across the room.

"What is wrong with you? I thought you said you were happy she was gone!" said Darin coldly.

"I never said that!" protested Daniel.

Mary turned away and put her head in her hands as she fought back tears.

"You're a liar!" said Darin.

"I am not! I just said I thought it

was probably for the best!"

Darin and Daniel tussled briefly, Daniel was pushed back and Darin stormed out of the room. "Some friend you are!" he yelled from down the hallway.

Mary fell to the couch as the tears came.

"I never said that, Mary," said Daniel. "You have to trust me. I never said it that way."

"It doesn't matter," said Mary as she cried. "It doesn't matter what you said or what he said you said or what he thought you said. What matters is what you feel right here and now."

Daniel clutched Mary.

"I love you, Mary. I don't know how or why and I don't know what tomorrow holds, but I love you. I really love you!"

Darin was agitated and angry. He slammed his apartment door and cursed Daniel. He felt betrayed. He had tried to get over the fact that Daniel was interested in his mother before, but now this! She was back, and in his arms.

And it was such a bad time. President McKinley had been making overtures about sending troops to Cuba. The little Civil War that was not much of a war at all was about to get a lot worse with American involvement. The paper had asked him to go back to Cuba a third time. He didn't need his best friend--his best friend!--pursuing his mother while he was gone.

Darin spent a sleepless night and then was off to work early April 11. Daniel was at the office, too, but they did not speak. Darin glared at him and Daniel turned his head.

Daniel couldn't help how he felt. Falling in love is not something he could control. It just happens sometimes and fighting it is impossible. He didn't plan it. He did not know why he felt so strongly about Mary, he just did.

Daniel looked across the office at Darin, busy writing headlines.

Darin shouted a headline out to the type composer. "*McKinley Vows To*

Send Troops And Arms To Cuba, Asks Congress For Money!"

"Use a slammer?" questioned the composer.

"Yes," Darin shouted back.

Daniel listened and tried to write his story, a sidebar about how many votes it would take Congress to approve appropriations to commit troops to Cuba. He knew the answer, but he couldn't think clearly. Before, he'd just yell the question to Darin and if he didn't know, someone else in the newsroom would. But now, Mary was a wedge between them. It was crazy, falling in love with his best friend's mother; with his co-worker's mother. Was it just lust? Did he really love her? Mary had spent the night in his apartment and he welcomed that. He wanted to be with her. She made him feel so invincible inside.

Yet, Darin would not even talk to him.

"*Navy Ready To Sail At Moment's Notice On President's Orders*," shouted Darin.

He was good, thought Daniel. That headline would sell lots of papers for sure.

Mary had straightened up the apartment by the time Daniel arrived home. Normally, Darin and Daniel would spend their evenings together, but Darin didn't even return to the apartment building. Daniel heard something about him going out on the town with other co-workers, but Daniel had not been invited.

Mary asked about Darin. Daniel told the truth. It wasn't good. The relationship was strained.

Mary lay her head on Daniel's chest as he gently caressed her forehead.

"I don't know why he can't be happy for us," said Daniel, "that we care for each other."

"He's reacting like any son would," said Mary.

"Yeah, like a complete ass."

"No," said Mary. "He's just trying to protect me."

"From me? That's a laugh," said Daniel.

"No, that's not what I mean. He's always been protective of me. He is the man of the family."

"He isn't acting like one."

"He'll come around."

Daniel snorted slightly. "You should have seen him at the office. We worked all day and not one word from him."

"What was he supposed to do?"

"Be civilized," said Daniel.

Mary turned and looked up at Daniel. "You know this is strange, you know it is."

"What?"

"You and me."

"I don't care. I can't help how I feel."

"Neither can I. I'm drawn to you and I don't really know why," confessed Mary.

"I didn't plan this."

"Nobody ever plans who they are going to fall in love with. But I felt it from the beginning. I felt it from the first day I met you."

"Me too," said Daniel.

As they held each other, their thoughts wandered. The problems of the world were forgotten. The time together was peaceful and both of them felt calm.

The conflict with Spain heated up and Congress did vote to appropriate funds to send troops to Cuba. By the middle of the month, resolutions were passed by Congress supporting the Cuban revolution and demanding that Spain withdraw from the island. The New York newspaper business went into overdrive. The less reputable papers greatly exaggerated the news, with wild headlines that the paperboys hawked on the street corners. A lot of money was made selling extra editions and circulation increased.

On April 23, Spain broke off diplomatic relations with the United States and formally declared war. "*War!*" was written across the *New York Empire's* front page in letters so big nothing else had to be said. By day Daniel worked the stories as they came in from reporters in Cuba and in Washington. By night, he and Mary took long walks in Central Park, cooked, talked, made love and had fun.

Darin was sent to Cuba again. Only a few words had been spoken between him and his mother.

The Cubans were greatly encouraged by the American support, but even then, the war was exaggerated. There was some shooting, but mainly shots fired in the night. Darin wrote headlines that were fairly accurate, but the bosses back home trumped them up. "*Two Dead*" was turned in to "*Enemy Forces Wiped Out*."

"*Shots Rang Out In The Evening*," became "*The Gun Battle Raged All Night*." What Darin and his fellow reporters saw was one thing. What the people of New York and around the country read was something completely different.

Mary worried. Though Daniel told her that his information was that the war was not all that bad, she believed the headlines. She prayed for Darin's safety and told Daniel how she worried.

It was terrible news when the telegram came to the office that Darin had been shot. Nobody there could believe it. They all knew the war was hyped up. Certainly it wasn't nearly as bad as they were saying. How could Darin actually get shot?

He was alive. But the shot to the chest was serious.

It was several days before Darin was brought back to a hospital in New York. The doctors were concerned that the swelling around his heart had not lessened significantly.

He was alert, but in a lot of pain, and when Mary and Daniel came to see him, he appeared ashen and distant.

Mary was a little surprised when she walked into the room. Her son, usually vibrant and full of life, was sickly and quiet.

"Hello, Mom," he said softly as he

reached his hand out to her.

"My baby," said Mary as she hugged him.

"Hello, Daniel," said Darin.

"What have you done with yourself?" asked Daniel.

"I guess I didn't see it coming. Supposed to duck, right?"

Daniel stepped up to the bed. "The war's gotten serious, hasn't it?"

"I guess that depends upon whether or not a bullet hits you," said Darin, smiling.

"Are you in pain?" asked Mary. She touched her son's forehead.

"Yeah," he said quietly, "a lot."

Mary looked at her little boy, her man, her only connection with Darby.

"I'm sorry, son," she said finally.

"About what?" asked Darin. Then he looked at Daniel with an anxious face. He understood what his mother meant.

"It's fine, Mom."

"I don't mean to hurt you," said Mary sincerely.

Darin looked at Daniel, then

touched his own chest and grimaced. The pain was pretty rough.

"Are you happy, Mom?"

"Yes, yes I am."

"Isn't that the most important thing?" he asked.

A tear slid from Mary's eye.

"I am happy." She reached and took Daniel's hand. "I know it is hard for you, but I am happy."

"That's what matters, Mom," said Darin. He reached up and dabbed a tear out of his eye.

"Daniel," he said a little louder. "I will kick your arse if you hurt my mother."

"I know," said Daniel. "I wouldn't have it any other way."

Mary cried that night. Daniel held her and it helped, but it didn't completely rid her of sorrow.

"I'm really scared," she said, as the two cuddled in the darkened apartment.

"I know," said Daniel. "I'm scared, too."

"I want someone to hold me and tell me it's going to be all right."

"I wish I could," said Daniel. "I wish I could say that and everything would be better."

"This is an overwhelming, crushing blow to my heart and soul," said Mary almost stoically. "I just can't do this."

"I'm here with you," said Daniel. "We can do it together."

"Love can be painful when it is lost. I love my son. I love you." She paused. "When I went back home, the thought of losing you was just too much," she said slowly.

"I missed you, too," said Daniel. "I wanted to be with you, to take you away."

"I don't want you to feel this sad, especially not ever because of me," she said.

"We'll get through this," said Daniel.

"My baby is so sick," Mary said almost silently. "God, please don't take my son. Please don't take Darby's son away from me."

Darin lay in the hospital for days. Mary and Daniel spent as much time with him as they could. The doctors were not optimistic. The bullet had nicked the heart and while they tried to make repairs in surgery, the technique was not the best and the young headline writer's heart showed terrible signs of infection and swelling. Fluid filled in around the heart and Darin struggled to breathe.

The war with Spain changed significantly May 1 when Commodore Admiral George Dewey of the U.S. Navy engaged the *Spanish Squadron.* The Battle of Manila Bay lasted several hours and left the Americans in charge of the waters. It was the first real shooting of the war that would last only into August.

The United States liberated Cuba, the Philippines, Guam and Puerto Rico from the Spanish. Spain's centuries long dominance of the oceans came to an end.

Darin did not live to see the war come to a close August 12. He died with his mother at his side and with Daniel nearby.

The doctors had told Mary that the end was near. Darin's heart was just not going to recover from the damage and the infection.

After he died, Mary went over her last words with him again and again.

He said he loved her and she told him that she would give him her heart. If *only* she could.

Weakly, Darin held his hands up as if writing a headline, "*Mom Gives Heart To Son*."

He smiled. "That would be something, Mom. That would really be something."

Mary did not know that she was pregnant at the time and so she never had a chance to tell her son that he would have a half brother. It would be a happy moment giving birth at her advanced age, but it was bittersweet without Darin.

Chapter 10

April 14, 1014

Dublin, Ireland

As frightening as it is to go into battle, Dubhghall could not get Meallan out of his mind. He really had no idea what would happen the following day and so it was important to him to keep his promise to his sweetheart. If it was at all possible to meet her next to the river he would do so.

As he left his friend Peadar behind, he weaved his way though the camp, thousands of men waiting restlessly for the coming day. All knew that it would be bloody the next day and that many would die. But Irish independence from the Vikings was essential and they were willing to make the sacrifice for their children and for future generations.

The air was heavy with smoke from campfires and the late night air was cool. Dub didn't recognize any of the men and they didn't know him. But he was with them and in a hurry to move away from the enemy, so no one questioned him.

Finally, he reached the edge of the camp where he looked both ways to see if anyone was really watching. They weren't, and so he took off at a trot. The river was just a mile away and he was to find a huge oak overhanging the river. There, Meallan had told him, she'd wait. Carefully, in the darkness, Dub slowed. He picked his way through the thick underbrush, eventually heard the river and he stopped.

Scanning about in the darkness carefully, the young farm boy looked for the tree. In the distance, he thought he saw it. He moved a few feet and then saw another tree that could be the meeting place, and then, another. He walked slowly. Thankfully there was a little moonlight reflecting on the water.

Dub felt nervous. But it wasn't nervousness about the coming battle, it was a good feeling, a feeling that he got when he was around Meallan. Funny about her, her father gave her a boy's name and pronounced it differently to make it her own. She was always special--special in a lot of ways, beautiful but assertive, innocent but strong. She stood up to people, and Dub loved that about her. She was all Irish--emotional and outspoken.

Dub stepped on a branch and it broke. A sound echoed out across the river. He stopped in his tracks and looked desperately along the bank of the river. There, he thought he saw a figure move. It had to be her.

He looked around and saw no one else.

"Psst. Meallan, is that you?" asked Dub.

Meallan called his name back.

"There is no one here," said Dub

softly, still in the darkness. "I checked all around."

They hugged and held each other tightly, spoke softly and slid in each other's arms to the base of the tree. They would be better hidden and could talk and tell each other how much they missed each other and about their love for one another. They listened to each other's heart beating for awhile. It was the essence of life and Dub felt Meallan's heart as he held her from behind.

Meallan gently stroked the back of Dub's hand with her thumb. It was a loving touch, an act of devotion.

"How do you feel?" asked Dub.

"I feel safe," she said quietly.

"I will keep you safe," said Dub.

"Why do you have to fight?"

Dub told her that soldiers had taught him how to fight and even though he was not a warrior himself, he would be behind the men with shields and axes--way behind. The enemy would have to knock them all down to get to him and that would never happen.

"It's dangerous," she said.

Meallan was worried and while Dub assured her that even the javelins could not reach his position and that King Brian would be there conducting the battle, she interrupted him.

"And you could be killed."

"Why do you say that?"

"I dreamed it," Meallan said softly.

"I'll be well."

"I swear I felt it. I dreamed that something awful will happen to you. You have to listen to me. You have to stand with your shoulder facing the Vikings. Always."

"Why?"

"You have to. In my dream you are hurt because you are standing facing the enemy. Please listen to me," pleaded Meallan.

"They will never get through the lines."

"But they do! I saw it. They will," said Meallan desperately. "Promise me you will listen to me."

Dub kissed Meallan on the back

of her ear.

"I promise."

Meallan picked up Dub's hand and directed it toward her breast.

They loved each other that evening out under the oak tree, and they bonded. For a short while there was nothing in the world except them. There was no war, no soldiers, no pain, no suffering of any kind.

Meallan looked up at Dub and gazed into his eyes. The moonlight reflected off her face and Dub could see her looking into his soul. She smiled.

"My spirit walks in the woods with you," she said.

"I will always be with you."

"*Look for me*," said Dub, "*I will find you*."

The battle that followed the next day was horrific. Men were sliced to pieces by heavy battle axes and rocks thrown from great distances caved in men's heads. Thousands were killed.

Dub fought so hard he thought he would pass out from exhaustion. His job was to hurl rocks over the heads of warriors on his side and hit those attacking. He was ordered to throw as many rocks on target as he could. He was good at that. He had hunted for food with rocks ever since his father taught him how. Stalk the prey slowly and throw a rock directly at their head. Animals would fall in one swoop.

But trying to kill men was different. They were armored and moving rapidly; they were angry.

As 13,000 men battled it out, Dub found his mind constantly thinking about Meallan and how much he loved her and how he would fight to protect her. He would find himself facing the enemy only to hear Meallan's words echo in his mind. He had promised to stand with his shoulder forward and so every time he thought of his promise to her, he would adjust his body.

Then, out of nowhere, a javelin came flying through the air. The Vikings had weakened the Irish line and were moving in fast. The javelin hit Dub and gouged out a hunk of flesh. The blood immediately came to the surface and Dub felt searing pain.

His head felt light and he looked over just as Peadar dropped to his knees.

'I want you to love me,' Meallan's voice said over and over in Dub's head.

"I do love you," he said. "I do love you. I will always love you. I will love you forever," he answered as the battlefield grew strangely quiet. He saw movement all around him but then it looked like a darkness came from beside his head out in front of him until it seemed like he was looking into a long black tunnel.

And then, it was dark and quiet and there was nothing but little footsteps he remembered making as a child. When or where he wasn't sure, but he somehow knew it was him. And then, nothing.

Ten thousand men were killed that day, hacked to pieces in a brutal slaughter. The Irish won. The Vikings were driven out of Ireland once and for all.

Death smells and it worsens by the day. Meallan searched the beach and the hills for two days. There were others looking, but not many. The horror was almost too much to bear.

Until, there, amid a pile of rocks, she saw Dub! She jumped to him and listened immediately to his chest. The blood had clotted. There was a shallow breath. There was a heartbeat!

She shouted for help. Two men came. Dub was alive. He was really alive!

When Dub saw Meallan, he struggled to speak. His eyes were distant, but he pushed out the words, "I did what you said. I did what I promised."

Meallan hugged him and held him as she sobbed.

Dubhghall and Meallan were eventually married and they had seven children--four handsome sons and three beautiful girls. Ireland was finally free and in the years ahead, prosperity spread throughout the country.

Chapter 11

Spring 1932

North Texas

When the stock market crashed on October 24, 1929, Black Thursday, leading to the infamous Black Tuesday on the 29th, the loss in wealth caused bankers and brokers and Wall Street types to leap to their deaths. There were those who were pleased by that news. Those who understood the Federal Reserve Act of 1913 were happy to see the financial markets finally crumble.

The Federal Reserve was nothing but a hoax, some said, a private banking cartel that partnered with Congress and duped President

Woodrow Wilson into the biggest American ripoff of all time. Seven New York bankers traveled secretly to Jekyll Island, off the coast of Georgia, in 1910, where they met for days to draft legislation. It was later rejected as being too probusiness Republican, so the bankers rewrote it slightly to make it appear more supportive of working Democrats. With that, and political shell games as to whom the real author of the legislation was, the bankers then sneaked the bill past Congress during the Christmas holiday on December 23, 1913, when a fair number of legislators were away.

Wilson backed the sinister plan because the bankers had given him money for his campaign during the election of 1912. And a sinister plan it was.

The Federal Reserve was a new Central Bank, the first in more than 80 years, and nothing but a group of private bankers, who would set the monetary policy of the United States by giving the Federal government "permission" to print money and then charge the government interest for the privilege. As it turned out, the Federal Reserve profited hugely from this paper money interest-creation plan, having no role in the actual printing of the money--since the work was performed by the U.S. Treasury. By controlling the money supply, the Federal Reserve controlled periods of boom and bust. They controlled lending and foreclosures, and they could sweep in huge volumes of wealth by setting predatory policies that were designed for self-benefit.

Looking ahead in 1910, the bankers at the Jekyll Island meeting even determined that the interest they would charge for giving the government permission to print their money, would create Federal debt that would never be paid off and for the government to even make gold bullion payments to the Federal Reserve, a new source of revenue had to be found. So, part of the plan was the 16th Amendment, creating a Federal Income Tax requirement. The 16th Amendment was more or less ratified by the States by February 1913, well ahead of the coming Federal Reserve. The ratification debate was lost in the shuffle and it never was quite clear if the amendment became a legal law or not.

Not since the temporary Revenue Act of 1862, pushed by Abraham Lincoln as an emergency measure to fund the Civil War, had anybody paid an income tax to the United States. Lincoln's tax law expired in 1872, and did not even affect most wage earning Americans, who then earned less than $600 per year.

But when the 16th Amendment came into being, for the first time in American history, most American citizens were expected to pay an income tax. What so many Irish immigrants had left Europe to escape, had raised its ugly head in the land of the free.

Income tax, the Federal Reserve, manipulated banking and lending, borrowing money to buy stock--these are the things that came together to create the Great Depression, spurred by the stock market crash of 1929, and suffered by the American people for twelve years. The bank runs and associated panic resulted from the realization that wealth stored in banks was not safe.

The common American in those years didn't understand the reasons for any of this. What news made it out of New York was only superficial, often exaggerated and certainly rewritten to blame the worldwide economic decline on someone else. World War I was just that; the blame game. World War II was on its way, born in the depression, and more of the same--blame someone else. The roaring 20s had come to a screeching halt, and there were those who blamed the problems on God's wish, a sort of punishment for the American decadence that surrounded an outright defiance of prohibition. It all led up to the crash. There were a lot of theories, some no doubt perpetrated by the rich bankers, to take the heat off themselves.

In North Texas, the farmers knew there was a depression on. But because they were generally self-sufficient, the long soup lines in the big cities did not reach the farm country. The farmers ate what they grew and while seeds seemed more scarce, and the price of goods was on the rise, the suffering did not really begin in earnest until the drought of 1931 and 1932.

"Marry me, Melissa," said Dean as he entered the Vernon Feed and Seed General Store, not far from Wichita Falls, Texas.

Melissa was a beautiful young woman, long red hair, freckles, huge eyes, eight years older than Dean.

She looked at the boy as he walked into the store sporting a cute smile. He was thin and tall, but Melissa was taller than him. His dark hair was unruly, desperately in need of grooming.

"Now why would I do that?" she returned.

"Just marry me," said Dean with a big smile. "We can figure out why, later."

"Do you have any idea how many

marriage proposals I get every day, young man?" replied Melissa with assertion.

"Well, let's see," said Dean as he put his hand up to his chin. "You run the Vernon Feed and Seed in the middle of a desert, you work here pretty much by yourself, there must be a few hundred farms that buy their seed here, every one of them has at least one single man looking for a wife. I'd say you get about a hundred proposals a month."

"That's about right," said Melissa with a big smile.

"So why don't you stop all those other guys and say 'yes' to me?"

"And break all those hearts?"

"Yes!" said Dean. "Shatter their hopes and dreams."

"You'd like that, wouldn't you?"

"What I'd like," said Dean as he leaned on the counter closer to Melissa, "is for you to marry me."

"I'm afraid I can't do that," said Melissa, "my father needs someone to run the store."

"What about your sister?"

"Aileen? Princess Aileen?"

"Yes, what about her?"

"She's 15 years old."

"And?"

"And, it takes a lot of responsibility to run this store, I'll have you know," said Melissa defensively.

Dean walked to the end of the counter and sighted along the top.

"What are you doing?" asked Melissa.

"Yes, yes this looks pretty good."

"What?"

"I think this counter would work."

"What are you talking about?"

"Nice and straight. Would take a little cutting and sanding."

"For what, Dean?" she said as her curiosity mounted.

"Or maybe we won't sand it. Leave it rough."

"Whaaat?"

"We could make a nice paddle out of this and spank that sister of yours. Spare the rod, spoil the child."

"You're crazy," laughed Melissa.

"Well, why can't she help out at the store? Fifteen is not too young."

"Maybe not for you," said Melissa.

"I'll have you know I am way past that age."

"You are not," smiled Melissa as she shook her head.

"I am." Dean held his chin up as if to be examined.

"You don't look a day over 15," said Melissa.

"I'll have you know I am 16 and I will be 17 before the year is out," he quipped.

Melissa laughed out loud. "I can see how you are stretching that."

"So how old *are* you?" asked Dean.

"I'm not telling you, and besides, don't you think you should know that before you ask me to marry you?"

"You don't look a day over 16."

"Ha, that would be something! I can tell you, I'm a lot more than a day over 16," said Melissa.

"So why don't you marry me?" asked Dean.

Melissa straightened some things on the counter. She picked up a wooden ruler and fidgeted with it. "You are persistent, I will give you that. You've been asking me to marry you for at least a year."

"And one of these days you'll say 'yes'."

"Don't you think we ought to maybe go on a date first?"

"Okay," said Dean. "Let me check my social calendar." He pretended to look at some imaginary papers in his hand. "I see, no, that won't work. Here, no. Wait, I can work you in on Friday."

"You wish."

"I do wish," said Dean as he stopped to look at Melissa more seriously. "If you won't marry me, go out with me."

Melissa looked at him without saying a word.

Dean looked back at her with anticipation.

"If I go out with you," said Melissa, "will you stop asking me to marry you every time you come into the store?"

Dean looked off up at the ceiling as if to think.

"No," he said. "That won't stop me. I can't make that promise. But there is something."

"What would that be?" asked Melissa.

"I will promise you that I will stop asking you to marry me if..." He let his voice trail off for emphasis.

"If what?" asked Melissa impatiently.

"I will stop asking you to marry me if you agree to say 'yes'."

Melissa smiled and turned to walk down to the end of the counter.

"I will give you one thing," she said finally, "Dean, you are the most persistent suitor I've ever known."

"Persistence is a good thing," said Dean. "You have to be persistent to be a farmer. That's how I got that 640 acres from the government. I agreed to farm it and they loaned me the money to buy it."

"Yes, you and every other farmer in this area," said Melissa with a change in mood. "It would be nice if there was a little bit of rain included in that deal."

"They told me there would be," said Dean.

"Seriously?" She was surprised.

"Yes, actually, they did, or the land man did. He said, and I will never forget the words, 'Rain follows the plow'."

"Oh, yes," said Melissa as she looked out the window to see the barren landscape. "That really worked out."

"Okay, so we're having a dry year," agreed Dean.

"A dry year indeed," returned Melissa. "I don't think it has rained enough to settle the dust in six months."

"But that doesn't mean it won't," said Dean.

Melissa sighed. "I hope you're right. Daddy says if we don't get some rain here soon there will be no point in planting and if farmers don't plant, we don't sell seed. The only thing left will be the grasshoppers and they'll starve."

"Funny you should say that," responded Dean, "I'm here for some wheat. I'm planting a hundred acres of wheat this year."

"That's a lot of wheat for one man," said Melissa.

Dean flexed his muscle and showed Melissa. "Not for a strong man like me."

Melissa smiled. "Yeah, you and your mules."

"And a finer animal God never made," said Dean. "With my plow and my mule team I can plow twelve acres in a week."

"I think not," said Melissa, smiling. "As dry as the ground is, those mules will drag you across the prairie and back again."

Dean chuckled. "Not if I crack the whip." He started surveying the counter again. "Or perhaps I'll make a paddle."

"Another Irish boy makes a fantastic claim."

Dean smiled from ear-to-ear.

"Is there anything, sir," said Melissa, "that I can do for you this morning?"

"I thought you'd never ask," said Dean, as he pulled a folded piece of paper out of his pocket. "You could start," he said, then hesitated as he studied the paper, "by marrying me."

"Oh, you," said Melissa playfully as she hit Dean's arm with the wooden ruler she had in her hand.

Dean moved back and laughed. "I just thought I'd ask."

Melissa prepared to write.

"All right," said Dean, "let me start with 125 bushels of wheat seed, assuming 10,000 seeds per pound, a half a case of O.K. Soap, a sack of Hi-Ball, a lantern, 5 gallons of fuel oil, a dust pan, two cases of Ball jars..."

"Hi-Ball or Snow Ball?"

"What's the difference?" asked Dean. "Hi-Ball's self-rising flour, that's what I want."

"Sure, but Snow Ball is too. They're both self-rising. The difference is Snow Ball makes a prettier bread," said the store clerk.

"Prettier bread? Now that should be something."

"No, really, it does. Snow Ball makes a very white bread."

"Oh," said Dean, "like snow."

"Just like snow," replied Melissa.

"I haven't seen any snow lately," said Dean, "no rain, no snow."

"Well, that's the difference."

"So how does it taste?"

"Like bread," said Melissa.

"That's good to know, it is flour after all," said Dean with some approval.

"I'm just telling you the difference."

"So which do you like better? I mean, if you're going to marry me, I want the flour in the house that you like."

"You don't quit, do you?" asked Melissa.

"I never quit," said Dean. "That

you will learn to appreciate."

"Snow Ball."

"All right, then Snow Ball it is, one sack. Or should we get two? Do you like to bake? I have a big cellar, dug it myself."

Melissa smiled. "Better get one. You can always come back for another later."

"Then one it is." Dean looked at his list. "Where was I?"

"A lantern and five gallons of fuel oil. And the canning jars. "

"You don't miss much, do you?"

"No," said Melissa. "Including that 10,000 seeds per pound business. What is that all about?"

"Well," said Dean, "I counted them."

"You counted them?" she said with surprise in her voice.

"Yep, counted five pounds of wheat seeds, 50,000 seeds. Counted a pound at a time and averaged the result. There are 10,000 seeds in a pound. It will take roughly 75 million seeds to plant 100 acres of wheat," said

Dean with authority.

"My, you figured that out?"

"I counted five pounds, averaged the outcome, did a little math and the answer is that if I want to plant 100 acres, it will take me 75 million seeds to do the job right."

"That's amazing," said Melissa.

"Seventy-five pounds per acre, 100 acres, 7,500 pounds, three trips to town, and I get to see you twice more, unless you decide to marry me first."

Melissa shook her head.

"So what made you count those seeds in the first place?"

"Well, simple really. I noticed that sometimes the seeds we get are bigger than other times. So, I wondered, how many seeds are there in a bushel? Come to find out, the bigger seeds broadcast better, seem to germinate with greater efficiency, and, it doesn't take as many per acre. So I like the big seeds, 10,000 per pound. I have to buy fewer seeds and I get a greater yield per acre. I make more money in the end, and therefore I get the farm paid off faster. So I will have to look at those seeds before I buy them from you."

"You know, Dean, I might just marry you after all. You're the most clever boy I've ever met."

"I told you."

Melissa grinned. "And you're cute, too."

Dean turned his head so Melissa could get a look at his profile.

"You are not like all the other men who ask me to marry them, that's for sure," said Melissa.

Dean finished dictating his shopping list, carefully examined the wheat seeds, and then helped Melissa find the other items and loaded them on his Model T pickup truck. The vehicle was a 1925 version, one of the 15 million that Henry Ford mass produced and sold for as little as $240 each. Dean's truck was a little beat up. He had bought it used for $50, but he was very proud to own it. All black with two seats and a generous pickup bed behind, it was the ultimate utility vehicle for farmers.

"This truck has a 177 cubic inch inline four cylinder engine," Dean told Melissa. "She gets 40 miles per hour and has the equivalent power of 20 horses all hitched in a row."

Melissa shook her head in amazement. Dean was an encyclopedia. He could throw facts and figures around all day long.

"Let me ask you something, Dean," said Melissa.

"What?"

"Is there anything you don't know?"

"Well, yes there is, actually," he responded. "I don't know what time you want me to pick you up this Friday."

Melissa tilted her head toward the porch floor, then pitched it up. "Assuming I were to go out with you, which I have not agreed to do, I think you should be at my house at 6 o'clock."

"And assuming you are not going to go out with me?"

"I think you should be there at 5:30, no later."

"All right, then, I will be there at 5:30 and I will wait until 6 o'clock to see what happens."

Melissa turned her head slightly, trying to conceal a smile. "We'll see," she said.

"Yes!" said Dean.

"Don't get too excited," said Melissa, "I did not agree to marry you."

"Not yet, but you will." Dean got into the truck as if to drive away.

"Aren't you forgetting something?" asked Melissa.

Dean looked at the load. He had his wheat and his flour and his fuel oil. He puzzled over it.

"That stuff isn't free," said Melissa.

"Oh, I'm sorry," said Dean. "I was distracted thinking about that wonderful date we are about to have."

"Well, come on inside and let's settle up."

Dean followed Melissa into the old clapboard building and walked across the wooden floor. He stopped to look at an orange and black box that had BOY SCOUT BROWNIE printed on it.

"What's this?" asked Dean as he pushed it a little.

"New Kodak," said Melissa.

"This is an empty box," said Dean as he picked it up and examined the image of a boy scout in uniform on the container.

"Actually the camera isn't in it," said Melissa. "It's a new model that is supposed to come out in October. They sent us that to help advertise. It will cost $2.00."

"Oh," said Dean. "I'd like to get one someday. I've always wanted to have a camera."

"A Boy Scout Brownie camera?" asked Melissa.

"Yes. I'm an Eagle Scout, you know."

"I did not know that."

"Yes ma'am, I am," he said with a huge grin. Melissa smiled back.

"And what would you do with a Boy Scout Brownie Kodak?" asked Melissa.

"Well," said Dean thoughtfully, "the very first picture I would take would be of you."

"You never quit, do you?"

"No. People who give up too soon don't succeed."

"I guess you're right," agreed Melissa.

"So when I get a camera, will you pose for me?"

"I certainly will," said Melissa as she tilted her head and blinked her eyes.

Dean's smile could not have been bigger.

"Too bad you don't have that camera now. I would buy it today."

"Have to wait on Kodak."

"That's too bad, because I would buy it with this order."

"Oh," said Melissa, who had been distracted from the task at hand. "One moment and I will have your bill totaled." Melissa looked at her list, totaled the bill and turned toward Dean.

"This is a lot of money."

"Not to worry," said Dean.

"You came into some cash?"

"Not exactly," said Dean. "The bank lent it to me. All I need, and then some."

"Well, that was nice of them," said Melissa.

Dean pulled a stack of bills out of his pocket and counted out what Melissa needed for the transaction.

"They sure make it seem easy," said Melissa.

"Who?" asked Dean.

"The banks. They're giving money to all the farmers."

"That's what makes the country run," said Dean.

"Well, it sure is helping Daddy's business."

"And the whole community will do well," said Dean, "once these crops come in. Then next year we will start over and farm even more acres."

Melissa wrote out a receipt and handed it to Dean.

"It is a pleasure doing business with you, sir," she said.

"The pleasure is all mine,

ma'am," said Dean. "I'll be at your house at 6 o'clock then?"

"Or 5:30," said Melissa with a smile.

"I can see you are going to be a hard one to win over."

"Maybe."

Dean looked at Melissa one last time.

"Well, I best be going. Got a lot of work to do today."

"Thank you, Dean."

"Thank you, Melissa."

Dean walked out the door with a spring in his step. When he got into the truck he looked back to see Melissa standing in the doorway watching him. He waved and she returned the gesture.

Dean was a worker, for sure. He drove back to his farm near Bugscuffle, unloaded the truck, stacked the grain in the shed, hitched the mules and plowed almost an acre before dark. He enjoyed Melissa and he was excited about finally getting to take her on a date. The question was, what should he take her to do? Should they drive into Wichita Falls and go to dinner? Maybe they could see a picture show. But would there be time to do both?

Dean was right on time at Melissa's house, 5:30. She wasn't ready, of course, but Aileen ushered him into the house and had him sit in the dining room as she announced to her sister that her gentleman caller was present. He had put on his nicest shirt and his newest trousers.

Dean could hear activity in the other room as the footsteps echoed on the wooden floor.

It was a nice house, tall ceilings, with huge windows. The windows were wide open and the warm breeze moved the white lace curtains ever so gently. There were transoms above the doors, so the house was well-ventilated. Dean heard a man's voice in the other room, probably Mr. McCarthy.

The young farmer tried to look at his reflection in a porcelain wash basin and pitcher. He could tell his image was affecting the light but he really couldn't see himself well. He smoothed his hair as a precaution.

Aileen came back into the room.

"Would you like a glass of water?" she asked shyly, offering Dean a glass. Aileen was not as tall as Melissa, but she was still taller than most girls. She was pretty, but not nearly as beautiful as her sister.

"Thank you very much," said Dean as he reached for the glass and took a sip.

"Momma says water is good on a day like this," said Aileen.

"Yes, it is," said Dean. "Cools you off."

"My sister says you're very cute."

"Oh, does she?" said Dean.

"She says you're smart, too."

"Well, you tell your sister that I appreciate her saying that."

"Run along," said Mr. McCarthy as he stepped into the room. Aileen left as Dean stood up and offered his hand.

McCarthy shook it. Dean had a strong grip because he was used to operating the plow. McCarthy noticed.

"I have not seen you in awhile," said McCarthy to Dean. Dean was a regular customer at the store.

"No, sir," said Dean, "Melissa has helped me the last few times. Did she tell you I'm planting a hundred acres in wheat?"

"No," said McCarthy. "That's quite a bit for one man."

"Well," said Dean nervously, "I have the mules."

"Thank goodness for the mules," said McCarthy.

"Yes, the mules, a finer animal God never made," said Dean.

"Yes, that's true," agreed McCarthy. He paused, looked at Dean, and Dean looked back awkwardly. Dean took another sip from his glass.

"Good water," he said.

"We could use some rain," said McCarthy with a sigh.

"Yes, we could," agreed Dean.

"I have not seen it this dry in a long time," said McCarthy. "Farmers are needing to plant, but we sure do need some rain."

"We do need rain," said Dean.

"Can't grow crops without rain," said McCarthy a little louder.

"Cannot grow crops without some rain, that's for sure," said Dean before he realized he was parroting McCarthy.

"Yeah, uh-huh," the older man replied, with a nod of his head. McCarthy walked to the front door and opened it. "Well, I best be going, have some chickens to pen."

"Goodbye, Mr. McCarthy."

"So long," said McCarthy as he closed the door.

Dean was relieved. He liked Mr. McCarthy well enough, but he was really nervous about the date and talking with Melissa's father seemed strained. He felt as if everything he said would be analyzed.

Melissa appeared at precisely 6 o'clock. Her beauty was striking. Dean looked at her and marveled. She did not look at all like the girl who served him at the store. She had fixed her hair with bobby pins and wore a beautiful silver necklace. Her dress was simple, but it looked freshly pressed.

"How do you do, sir?" she said.

"I am doing well," said Dean, mustering his best manners. "I must say, ma'am, you look well-favored."

"Well-favored?" asked Melissa with a smile.

"That is to say," Dean groped for the biggest word he could think of, "that is to say, you look exquisite."

"Why, thank you, Dean. I must say you look rather handsome yourself."

Dean escorted Melissa out to the truck and they drove to Wichita Falls. The air was hot, and so Dean fumbled with a piece of wood he had fashioned to fit onto the door and direct wind into the cab. He had built it for his side but was able to set it up where air was directed toward Melissa.

"That's very clever," said Melissa as she let the wind blow on her face. "Cools me down." Dean smiled at her proudly.

Dean did not know Wichita Falls

well, but he found Main Street and spotted a little diner on the corner near the courthouse. It was a small shop, but inside, there were a dozen tables, most of which were empty. Clearly the diner could have used more business than they were getting on a Friday night. Dean asked the waitress about it and was told business had been pretty slow.

The meal was served promptly. Melissa and Dean had pork chops, cooked lettuce, parsley potatoes, fresh bread and coffee. The food smelled great and was filling. As Dean paid at the counter, he spent a nickel more for a new candy, the *3 Musketeers* made of fluffy chocolate, strawberry and vanilla nougat. He shared it with Melissa and she told him she had never tasted anything so delicious before.

"That Mr. Mars can make some candy, can't he?" asked Dean.

"Yes he can," agreed Melissa.

The clerk had given Dean a nickel change and instead of putting the buffalo nickel in his pocket, he rubbed the shiny 1928 coin and presented it to Melissa.

"A beautiful coin for a beautiful girl," he said as he offered it to Melissa.

Melissa smiled and at first didn't take the coin.

"Go ahead," said Dean. "Keep it as a reminder of the most wonderful date of all time."

Melissa took the coin and examined it.

"Nineteen twenty-eight?"

"No," responded Dean. "Us, our date."

Melissa laughed, "I know what you meant."

"Besides," said Dean, "someday they will quit making those."

"No, they won't," protested Melissa.

"Yes," said Dean philosophically, "I think they will."

"You're so silly," said Melissa, as she put her arm around Dean's waist.

The picture show was not far from the town square and while there were several dozen people gathered to see the movie, it wasn't crowded.

The movie was *Anna Christie*, starring Greta Garbo and billed as Garbo's first talking picture. Dean found it to be a little boring, but Melissa loved it. It was fascinating to see actors actually talk in films, but Dean didn't find the plot all that engaging.

Part way through the show, Dean reached over and picked up Melissa's hand. He was nervous about it, but she responded and they held hands the rest of the movie. Melissa even leaned her head on Dean's shoulder. Had she not done that, he might have enjoyed the movie better, but with her so close, he was distracted and could not concentrate on Greta Garbo--with or without sound.

Melissa had a wonderful time with Dean, and told him so on the porch when he dropped her off. That was just the beginning, and their dating led to marriage two months later. Dean was right, Melissa couldn't say "no" forever.

Dean planted his 100 acres,

worked from dawn to dusk, plowed and chopped and spread the wheat seeds with consummate care. There were a few light rains as the spring turned to summer, but not nearly enough for a fledgling crop.

The seeds sprouted, some of them anyway, but the stalks blistered as they pushed out of the earth into the sun. It was brutally hot.

Sometimes the winds would blow and the dust clouds that could be seen in the distance seemed to stretch for miles. They deposited a fine red dust everywhere. It was a powder that got into everything and was impossible to clean away completely.

Melissa was a good wife--she baked bread, washed clothes, kept the house clean when Dean was out working. He would always come in hungry and she would make sure he had a good meal.

Dean was optimistic by nature, but nature was not treating the farm well. The hand dug well was looking deeper and deeper as the water table fell. The water itself was not as clear as before and what little rain fell did not seem to replenish it.

Mr. McCarthy made Aileen work in the store. She did not enjoy herself, but she had no choice. Business got worse as farmers lost hope in having a crop.

Dean had been talking about buying a windmill for the well, but the prospect was expensive and the bank money was running out.

Dean did have a series of wooden rain barrels that he used to collect rain off the roof, but there wasn't enough rain to keep them even partially filled.

Melissa detected that Dean was getting despondent. He worked harder than any man she knew. But making crops grow when there was no water was an impossible undertaking. The wheat stalks that did make it to the surface often turned crispy and eventually died. Dean tried to baby them, but it was useless.

The bank called a big meeting in

Vernon and farmers from all around traveled to hear what was to be said.

There were not going to be any crops in that area in 1932, and everyone knew it. The bank had lent all the farmers money and with little or no prospect of making anything on a crop, there wasn't much hope of repaying the loans on a timely basis.

The farmers were pretty angry when the man from the bank told them that they needed to come up with the money to repay the bank, or the bank would have to start calling in some of the loans.

"Just how are we supposed to come up with the money?" asked one old-timer sitting in the front row of a very crowded meeting room. "You all gave us this here money and told us we didn't have to pay it back until the crops were sold."

"That's what you told me, too," shouted another man from back in the audience.

"What are we supposed to do if there ain't no rain?" asked still another.

The banker seemed unsympathetic. He was told by his bosses to get the money. They didn't tell him how, and if he didn't come up with the money, they would start the foreclosures.

"We'll accelerate the maturity of the loans," he said finally.

"What the hell does that mean?" asked the farmer in the front row.

"It means," said a man sitting not far from him, "that if you don't make payments and I mean right now, they want all the money you borrowed instead."

"That's crazy," came a shout from the back. "If I don't have the money to make payments, how the Hades am I going to pay the whole God-forsaken amount?"

There was grumbling and jeering.

"It is out of my hands," said the banker.

Dean stepped into the center where he could be recognized.

"Why were ya'll so anxious to

give us this money when you knew darn well it would take us a few years to pay it back? It's not like everyone here has been sitting around doing nothing." There was approval in the crowd.

"We work hard," gestured Dean, pointing around the room. "All of us do. Do you think we want our hard work to go to waste? We plowed, we bought seed, we planted. God just didn't give us the rain."

There was applause.

"I understand that," said the banker over the noise. "I know all of you. I've talked to each one of you individually. The bank had the money to lend. But the bank needs that money to be paid back. You have to make payments."

"There is no money," a man hollered. "Don't you see? The crops failed. All the crops failed. It's drier than hell out there. God, the dust storms are getting worse, the land is blowing away. Most of my seeds got sucked up into the sky."

"That's right!" said another man.

"I'm just telling you," said the banker with noticeable anger in his voice, "they want me to get the money and if I don't, they're going to start taking farms."

"The farms we worked," said Dean. "The houses we built, too? What about our sweat? Is the bank going to pay us for that? All the bank did was give us money for materials. We did the work. Look around here. These men did the work. You take their farms and you're stealing their labor."

The crowd burst out with approval. The banker packed up his leather satchel.

"That's all I have to say," he said as he headed for the door.

The summer was awful. North Texas climate was unbearable when there was no rain. The temperature rose soon after the sun made its appearance in the morning and it seemed to just get hotter as the day wore on. It was like standing in a hot oven. Even being in the shade was uncomfortable.

The house that Dean had built on the farm was not very big, but it was a good house. The siding was shiplap, whitewashed to protect the wood. The wooden shingles had faded in the sun. It only took one season to change the fresh new wood into a slate grey.

There was a porch on the front of the four room building. It was a good place to sit in the afternoons when the sun was behind the house. Dean had also built a barn where he stabled the mules, a nice outhouse, and he had a deep well and a root cellar. He kept potatoes in the cellar, with his canned goods. It was always cooler underground. There were chickens for eggs and a small goat for milk. It was a modest place, but Melissa adopted it as her home when she married Dean and she was happy to live there.

The prospect of maybe someday losing it was bothersome to them both.

When the first letter came, demanding money for the loan, Dean and Melissa placed it on the kitchen table as a reminder. There was a layer of dust that had been deposited from the previous night's winds and Dean wiped his hand across the table to clean a spot.

"There's no way they will take this farm," announced Dean. "You know they don't want the farm. They would rather me work and pay them back. What use is a farm to the bank?"

"I know," said Melissa. "It doesn't make any sense, unless they want to take it back just so they can sell it again to the next farmer."

"They know I'll work until I pay them back. They know that about me."

Melissa sat in the wooden chair beside Dean and pulled it up close. Perspiration beaded up on her forehead. "I know you will." She held Dean's hand. He looked at her.

"Thank you for marrying me," he said.

"I love being married to you," she replied, softly.

Dean picked up the letter and then flipped it back onto the table.

"Why did you marry me, Melissa?" he asked after a brief silence.

"I married you because I fell in love with you."

"But you could have married anybody."

"I didn't want just anybody. I waited for you to come along and I picked you. You're the one I want to be with."

"But you told me 'no' for a year," said Dean.

"I was just making sure you were serious," she said as she pulled Dean's hand a little closer.

Dean smiled. "I was serious the first time I asked you," he said.

Melissa looked into his eyes. "I know. I could tell."

"And you trusted me to take care of you."

"You are taking care of me," she said.

"But what if we lose the farm?"

"So? It's just a farm."

"But it's our farm," said Dean.

"Yes it is. But we will always have each other. No matter what happens, we will always be together. Nothing can separate us."

Dean leaned over to his wife and kissed her.

"I love you," he said.

That night, the two took a blanket Melissa had sewn and spread it out in front of the house so they could lay down and look at the stars.

The night sky was incredible. There were billions of stars visible and the Milky Way seemed so clear it was like a cloud blowing across the sky. The moon had set and so the night was dark and each star twinkled with such purity that looking up at them was like flying among them. Little did they know that just a few hundred miles west of them in Roswell, New Mexico, there was a man by the name of Robert H. Goddard who had lain with his wife, Esther, many times, on a blanket, looking up at the night sky, dreaming of someday flying there. Goddard was a professor from Worcester, Massachusetts, who had moved to Roswell to pursue his rocket experiments with liquid propellent engines. An unknown pioneer,

Goddard was also hard hit by the depression and had flown his last rocket April 19, 1932, before his funding from the Harry Guggenheim Foundation was suspended. Even famed aviator Charles Lindbergh would one day fly to visit Goddard and pass through the very sky that Dean and Melissa looked at from their place.

It was such a beautiful sight and as the couple reclined together, their cares seemed to disappear. How could something so beautiful not make you feel somehow connected to it all? Dean put his feet up in the air.

"What are you doing?" asked Melissa.

"Look, put your feet up with me." She did. "It's like we're walking up there."

Melissa laughed. "You are so crazy."

Dean put his feet down and rolled over toward Melissa. She clamped her legs around his.

"But you love me, though, don't you?"

"I love you because you are crazy," said Melissa. "I love snuggling with you." Melissa moved where she could rest her head on Dean's powerful shoulder. "I love you with all my heart and soul and I will love you forever. You'll never have to look for me because I will always be by your side."

Dean kissed her. "You're so pretty," he said.

There was no light but Dean could make out her outline.

"You can't even see me," she said.

"I don't have to see you. I know you are the prettiest girl in the whole country." He kissed her again slowly.

"Look! Did you see that?" exclaimed Melissa.

"No."

"Wow," said Melissa. "That was the biggest shooting star I have ever seen. The trail went all across the sky."

"Make a wish," said Dean.

"Humm, let's see, I wish to be in your arms for the rest of my life."

"You're not supposed to say it out loud," said Dean. "For it to come true it has to be a secret."

"I don't want to keep that a secret."

Melissa shouted out, "I love my husband and I want to spend the rest of my life with him and be in his arms forever!"

"Well, now the neighbors know it," said Dean playfully.

Melissa laughed. "Neighbors? We don't have any neighbors. You can walk five miles in any direction and there are no neighbors."

"Well, in that case," said Dean as he shouted, "I love my wife and I will be with her until the end of time!"

There was silence. Then a mule stirred in the barn.

They both laughed. Dean started and Melissa helped him finish his sentence, "A finer animal God never made."

Dean reached up and unfastened the buttons on Melissa's dress. She unbuttoned those on his shirt.

"You're a wonderful man," she whispered. "It's hard to keep my hands to myself."

Dean kissed Melissa's chest.

"I see you being in the rest of my life," she said. "No matter what happens."

Three more weeks passed before the next letter arrived. It was hard not knowing what was going to happen. There was certainly no wheat in the field and Dean had tried scratching around to find and recover seeds that did not sprout. He had picked up almost a bushel. Maybe, he thought, he could plant them next year and get some kind of yield.

In the distance, there were noises. Another windstorm was kicking up, and way off on the horizon, Dean could see the sky darken. He walked the long distance from the house out to the road where the letter carrier had made the mail run. All around, Dean could see only dry land. The 100 acres he had planted had dead, dry, twisted sprouts. The 540 acres he had not plowed had dead range grass. The land next to his was the same thing. The land across the dirt road was similar. It was so dry there weren't even any grasshoppers anymore. And the dirt had a particular dry smell. It was dusty, too. Each footstep left a little cloud. If ever a car drove by, the dust that got kicked up lingered. Dean's hands were dry and dust always clogged his nose. He wondered, why was he there? Why was anybody there? There used to be a cattle trail that went through Vernon years ago, but all that ended when motorcars were invented. Cattle were hauled a lot by rail, too, through Ft. Worth and what once was a thriving trail-driving economy had given away to economic desolation.

Dean carried the letter to the root cellar to read it. It was cooler, and quiet. He called out for Melissa, who was in the house.

Seated at the bottom of the ladder that led into the cellar, Dean opened the envelope slowly.

The letter was bad. It stated that some trust company was now the rightful owner of the farm--the farm, and all the improvements--the house, the well, the barn. Dean could not believe what he read.

Melissa came to the cellar and looked through the open door.

"What is it, Dean?"

Dean held up the letter without speaking. Carefully, Melissa stepped down the wooden rungs. She could see by Dean's face that the news was not good. She recognized the envelope as being from the bank.

"What does it say?" she asked.

Dean held it up. "They took the farm," he said matter of factly. "They took the farm, the house, everything."

"They can't do that," said Melissa solemnly.

"It says here that some trust company in New York City is the 'rightful owner' of our land. I don't even know who these people are."

"Rightful owner?" asked Melissa. "What does that mean?"

"It means they took the farm," said Dean, "just like they said they would."

"But how can they do that?"

Dean handed the letter to Melissa. "They accelerated the maturity of the loan."

"How can they do that?"

"They just did," said Dean angrily. He punched the dirt beside him.

Melissa sat in Dean's lap as a tear dripped out of her eye.

"They can't do this."

Dean hugged Melissa and held her. She felt thin to him. She had lost weight, as had he. Times were hard enough, barely living, hoping and praying every day for rain, not eating enough--that was the normal course. And then, to have some New York banking trust take their land and their house! It was overwhelming.

Outside, the wind picked up and dirt fell in through the open cellar door. Melissa jumped up and pulled the door closed. Dean pulled the rope and tied it to an inside support post.

The wind started to blow hard.

"Oh," Melissa said abruptly. "All

the windows are open in the house. There's going to be dirt everywhere!"

Dean looked through a crack in the door. The wind was blowing hard and red dust partially obstructed the view of the house. A little sunlight made the dust glow inside the cellar.

"Well, then we will just have to clean it when this is over."

"No, let me go shut the windows," said Melissa.

"Not now," said Dean. "It's too windy."

"I'll run fast and come back."

Dean put his arm out to prevent Melissa from going up the ladder.

"It's going to be a mess in the house," said Melissa sternly.

"I don't care. That wind's bad," said Dean. "We're safer down here."

Dust blew in through the cracks in the door and the sunlight was blocked out. What was once day turned into night. It was impossible to see the house. The constant blasting of dirt against the old wooden door grew louder and louder until it was almost a roar.

"Why's it so loud?" asked Melissa.

"Don't know," said Dean in a raised voice. "We better get down." Dean stepped back down the ladder and tugged on Melissa's hand. She was following him when suddenly, the door was ripped off the root cellar and in a cloud of dust she was pulled out of Dean's grip. He scrambled up the ladder.

"Melissa!" he shouted. "Melissa!"

The wind and dust was so bad that it was impossible to see anything. There was a crashing noise and the breaking of glass and one of the mules made an awful sound.

Dean's eyes filled with dirt and his heart panicked. He couldn't see Melissa and called her name again and again and again. Debris hit him in the face and bloodied him. Desperate, he tried to stick his head outside and was almost sucked away himself.

"Melissa!" he shouted. "Melissa!"

The wind continued to blow, but

the roaring sound that took the house, the truck, the barn, the animals, and Melissa, died down after a few minutes. Dean could not see, his eyes torn by dirt, his face raw.

It was a monster tornado that took everything from Dean in a few seconds. It was God's wrath.

Dean's heart was in agony, and when the wind finally did slow, he looked in shock out over what used to be his farm. There was nothing left there for the bank to take. Nothing.

Dean left the cellar and searched for Melissa even before all the wind had stopped. He walked miles, longing for her, in despair. "*I will find you*," he kept saying, "*I will find you*."

Dean had tried to find wood to build a shelter after that, but he ended up living in the root cellar, eating what food was there, and grieving.

Dean quit eating after that and within three months, still 16 years old, he was dead. It was starvation, or a broken heart, or both. He just could not live without his beloved Melissa.

Chapter 12

December 7, 2008

Canyon Lake, Texas

The rain came down so hard that it whipped up against the huge picture window in Wallace's study and he and Lauri could barely see out into the yard. The wind blew, and leaves were ripped off branches as they were tossed around.

"I can't believe this," said Lauri. "I have never seen it rain so hard!"

"I think we are getting the outer bands of a tropical depression," said Wallace.

"This late in the year?"

"Well, I don't know," said Wallace, "it just seems like it."

"Don't you ever worry that that window will come crashing in?" The lights flickered as thunder cracked violently.

"Yeah, it seems like it, but it's tempered glass. It's supposed to handle stuff like this."

Lauri stepped away from the glass just in case. She sat in the recliner next to where Wallace was sitting.

Wallace sipped from a mug of hot chocolate.

"Did you touch the glass?" asked Wallace.

"No."

Wallace got up, felt the glass and then sat back down. "It's getting cool out there, too."

"Cold front, then," said Lauri.

"Maybe."

Lauri looked over at Wallace. "What if this is the end of the world?"

Wallace smiled. "What if?"

"Well, it could be, you know. It could rain for forty days and forty nights and drown us all."

"I don't think so," said Wallace.

"Why not?"

"Well, for one thing, the Bible says that's never going to happen again."

"Okay, so suppose it rains for thirty-nine days and nights?" quipped Lauri.

"Well, then I think we better get our swim fins out."

Lauri smiled. She liked Wallace. He was easy to talk with and though sometimes the conversations were meaningless, he still made it fun. She had been living at his house since coming home from the hospital and she didn't want to leave. She had brought a lot of her things over from her place. They had never actually discussed how long she'd stay, but she thought that eventually maybe the subject would come up and she didn't know how to handle it.

She had been having some pretty dramatic nightmares, or dreams, or premonitions. She wasn't sure what they were. Wallace was always there to listen. He didn't have the answers she wanted, but he made her feel as though perhaps they could figure out what was happening with her.

She also began seeing things in the house. She referred to them as entities. Sometimes they were very scary and she reached to Wallace for comfort. Sometimes they were non-threatening. She felt strong emotions at times, associated with some presence, or some memory or some glimpse into the future. At times she would cry for no apparent reason.

Wallace noticed her looking out the window deep in thought.

"What are you thinking about?" he asked finally.

"Oh, just things," she said.

"Things you feel?"

"Yes," she said.

"Anything in particular?"

"No, just that I feel like I'm going insane," replied Lauri.

"You're not insane if you think you're insane," said Wallace. "It's the people who swear that they are sane who turn out to be insane."

Lauri looked at Wallace out of the corner of her eye.

"I'm serious."

"I am, too," said Wallace. "Have you ever heard of a schizophrenic listening to voices who goes around claiming he's insane? No, it doesn't happen. He may be as nuts as they come, but he is going to swear that there is nothing wrong with him. Yet the voices tell him what to do and drive him over the edge."

"I see."

"That's the point. If you are sane and you occasionally question your sanity; think you are a loon because you don't understand something, that's a sign that you are, in fact, sane."

"How do you know all this?"

"I just studied it, that's all. And I've talked to a lot of people who were perfectly sane who felt they were losing their marbles."

Lauri smiled. "Losing their marbles, nuts, loons, you're funny."

She made a funny voice, "I hear voices and they don't like you."

Lauri reached her hand over the armrest and picked up Wallace's hand. "Do you think we're both crazy for feeling these past lives?"

"I don't know. I can't explain it. That doesn't mean it isn't real," said Wallace.

"What did you think when I kissed you in the cemetery?" asked Lauri softly.

"I thought you were crazy," the psychologist said, with a smile.

Lauri looked at him with a puzzled look on her face. "I'm trying to be serious."

"Okay," said Wallace, as he turned to face Lauri more squarely. "I was in pretty bad shape. I mean, I was really going to do myself in. I had given up. I didn't want to live. And then, out of nowhere, you showed up. I had no idea where you came from, why you were there. But all of a sudden, you took charge. You put your head down next to mine and you just basically freaked me out of pulling the trigger. I didn't want to kill you just because I didn't want to live. Because you did that, you saved me. And now, it seems as if together, we have some kind of purpose."

"So what did you think when I kissed you?"

"Well, it was strange. A thing like that happens once in a million years. I thought you were like an angel or something."

"A guardian angel?"

"Yeah, and right when you kissed me, I mean I didn't know you at all, three words went through my head," said Wallace. "I have no idea why that happened, but in my mind I said, 'I love you'." Wallace paused.

"And?"

"I didn't say it out loud, but I thought it. And it was as clear as could be. I never even saw you before but I felt this sense of love for you."

"Then, we kissed again," said Lauri, "and we had those thoughts."

"Yes!" said Wallace. "We had that flood of thoughts and what was strange is that you and I had exactly the same thoughts. That kind of thing doesn't happen."

"But it did," said Lauri. She moved closer to Wallace.

"Yes, it did." Wallace stopped talking. Lauri leaned closer until she kissed Wallace. They both felt an energy flow between them.

Suddenly, Lauri gasped and pulled away.

"What?"

Wallace looked stunned.

"Did you get that," asked Lauri.

"About Dub and Meallan?"

"Yes!" said Lauri. "Did you feel that?"

"That he wasn't killed in the battle?" asked Wallace.

"Yes! Yes! They got the message!"

"I can't believe this," said Wallace.

"They got my message," said Lauri with excitement. "I told him to jump to the left. He didn't die!"

Wallace leaned back in his recliner and grasped both armrests.

"This is incredible!"

"Incredible?" asked Lauri. "Are you kidding me? We communicated with one of our past lives. We actually talked to them!"

"Well, you talked to them," said Wallace, "I just put you into hypnotic regression."

Lauri leaned back in her chair. "My mind is blown. My mind is completely blown."

Lauri jumped out of her chair and straddled Wallace in his chair. She grabbed him and kissed him deeply.

For the first time, during their embrace, they saw images of Dean and Melissa and a glimpse of Mary breaking off the wedding from Robert.

Lauri pulled back. The two looked into each other's eyes.

"This is insane. Now this is the definition of insane," said Lauri.

"Did you see a girl named Melissa?"

"I'm Melissa," said Lauri. "I'm Melissa and it hurt like hell when I got sucked into that tornado."

"I don't believe this," said Wallace, dumbfounded.

"Hypnotize me," said Lauri with excitement. "Hypnotize me right now. Maybe I can help them."

"Do you have any idea what you're saying?"

"Yes! You know what I can do. I can really do these things."

Wallace shook his head from side-to-side. "I hear what you are saying, but I don't believe it."

"You felt it." Lauri smooched Wallace again.

"Okay," said Wallace finally. "I believe you. Well I've always believed you. But I don't understand it."

"What's to understand? We are in touch with our past lives and we can change things!"

"That's just impossible," said Wallace. "Scientifically impossible."

Lauri leaned back and stared at Wallace with a look of mild disapproval.

"Impossible?" she asked slowly.

"What do we really know about anything? How do we know that we aren't some kind of guardian angels for them? How do we know we don't have this power to protect them, to protect us?"

"Whoa," said Wallace. "Okay, I, I'm with you. If we can do this, I guess they will put us on Oprah."

Lauri was giddy with delight. She was like a child discovering a new sensation.

"Okay, hypnosis it is. But we have to figure out what we are going to try to communicate."

"Let's help Melissa. Let's make sure she stays in the root cellar and doesn't get sucked away."

"How are we going to do that?" asked Wallace.

"I suppose I'll tell her to be afraid, to make her stay away from that door. Both of them. They need to crouch way down in the bottom of the cellar so they won't get hurt."

"Good enough," agreed Wallace.

Lauri climbed onto the couch and leaned back to relax. Wallace sat beside her and asked her to relax and to concentrate on her outstretched hand.

In a few minutes, Lauri was in a hypnotic trance. Wallace directed her back to the root cellar and to Dean and Melissa.

Lauri felt her mind start to move. At first she perceived a long tunnel. She saw flashes of light coming in from openings in the side but she could not determine what they were. Once, she saw herself walking down the tunnel. She stopped, and looked at herself. It was a weird feeling, to be able to stop and look at yourself from outside your own body.

She heard Wallace's voice, encouraging her to find Melissa. Then, she moved down the tunnel again and came out onto the North Texas prairie. She saw a huge dust cloud in the distance, approaching her fast. She felt fear. She said "be afraid" to herself. She looked in different directions, searching, searching, looking for the house.

Instantly Lauri was in the root cellar. Dean was reading the letter from the bank. Melissa came to the opening above ground. "What is it, Dean?" she asked.

Lauri concentrated. *Be afraid*, she thought with all her might. *Hide from the storm. Get down. Stay away from the door.*

Lauri heard Wallace's voice again. He was talking in a monotone. "You can feel fear. You can project that fear to Melissa."

Lauri saw the tunnel again; she felt it closing in on her. She started to feel a lot of anxiety. Her heart beat wildly. She moved on the couch suddenly.

"Are you okay, Lauri?" asked Wallace. "You are fine. You are here with me. Nothing can hurt you. You hear the sound of my voice and everything is all right."

Lauri started to relax a little. Her mind continued to wander, but not toward the root cellar. There was something else, but she was not sure what. She could hear Wallace's voice but it began to fade. The tunnel closed in on her. It felt tight. Lauri couldn't breathe. She saw herself scream but didn't hear the sound.

There was David Ross, sitting on a couch, smiling at her, holding his hand out to her. She reached toward him. But, before she touched him she was pulled back rapidly. Faster and faster, his image got smaller and smaller and smaller. "Help," she thought. She wanted to wake up, but she couldn't. Where's Wallace? She couldn't hear Wallace. "Wallace!" What's happened to Wallace?

Chapter 13

1957

Hollywood, California

David didn't know what to do about Misty. He loved her dearly but could not seem to get through to her. Her self-destructive personality was slowly killing her. She complained that she did not know what day it was, couldn't remember conversations she had just had. She had even forgotten the times they made love. He thought they were special. She couldn't even remember them.

He hoped that he could somehow get her off the drugs and alcohol. But it was pretty hopeless. She felt she needed them to feel alive, when the fact was, she used them to stay numb.

A great talent, he thought, wasted. He brought her back from the brink of despair one time, orchestrated her come-back. But as soon as the bright lights faded, so did she.

She loved it when she worked, but when the cameras were gone and the lights were gone and when the attention was on someone else, she was devastated. David tried. He tried, and tried and tried. If he could just get her out of the house, out of bed, out of her rut, she'd be all right, he thought. Hope springs eternal.

What made her special, he didn't know. Why she suffered such turmoil he did not understand. Odd how he had even gotten to know her. It was a once in a lifetime chance that he even ran into her on the beach, and that she liked him and that she was willing to work with him. He certainly never dreamed he'd end up living with the famous Misty Adams. She could have had anybody. But he was there with her. Why? Why him?

David felt inadequate. She didn't listen to him, didn't change, didn't see the light. It was as though her destiny was already determined.

"Misty, let's go for a drive," he said one afternoon. She was still in her nightgown, still in bed. "Misty?"

David knocked lightly on the bedroom door and pushed it open.

She looked terrible. Her eyes were vacant and the bags under them were dark and pronounced. She wasn't eating and looked bony and frail. The curves that the world so loved were shrinking away.

"Misty, let's take a drive," said David. "Let's go to the coast."

Misty groaned.

"Why?" she said.

"C'mon, Misty. Go with me. I don't want to go alone."

Misty turned and looked at David.

"Why do you love me, David?" she asked.

"Why shouldn't I?"

"Just leave me," she said. "I

don't want to go out today."

"I need you with me," said David.

"I'm nothing but trouble for you. Just go without me."

"No, Misty, it will be good for us both."

Misty reached to her nightstand and fumbled for a bottle of pills.

"My head hurts."

David watched her feel around for the bottle. It tipped off the table and rolled.

"Oh, God." she said as she heard the bottle hit the floor. "Get that for me, David, please."

"No, Misty. You don't need that. Let me get you some aspirin."

"Aspirin! I don't need any aspirin. I need my medicine."

"Medicine?"

"Where's my drink?" asked Misty. She leaned up in bed and took the last swig out of an open bottle.

David leaned against the wall. The bottle of pills had rolled and touched his foot. He lightly kicked the bottle. Misty didn't notice as she flopped back in bed.

David sat on the bed beside her and caressed Misty's head.

"Come with me to the coast," he said. "We can watch the sunset together."

"Why today?"

"Why not today, Misty? Why not start today to change all this? You know how much you love the water. We can go skinny dipping after dark."

Misty smiled.

"You remember."

"Of course I remember. That was a very special evening for me."

"Tell me, David, did we have sex that day?"

"No, Misty, you know that. You've asked that before."

"That's why I fell in love with you. You're not like all the other men I've known. They just want one thing. And you're different."

"Different David," said David. "I know, that's what you call me. That's what you've always called me."

"Because you are. You *made* me love you. You treated me like a lady. You've always treated me so well."

David rubbed Misty's head. Her eyes closed slowly. David caressed her neck and her shoulders.

"That feels wonderful," she said softly.

"We're just two people," said David.

"We were meant to be together," said Misty quietly. "I'm so lucky to have met you."

"Misty?" asked David quietly. "If something happened to me, would you miss me?"

"Yes!" she said soundly.

"Would you really miss me?"

"If something happened to you," she said, looking up at him, "it would break my heart."

David smiled.

"I kinda thought you would say that."

"Why do you ask that? You know I love you."

"I'm just wondering." He paused. "I couldn't bear to lose you either." Misty looked at him with admiration.

"I just want to help you so that you can enjoy all the good things in life, things you deserve."

David moved both of his hands onto Misty's breasts and caressed them gently.

"Oh, God," she said with an approving sigh. "That feels so good."

"Go with me today."

Misty smiled. "Okay," she said after a long pause. "I'll go to the beach as long as you promise to never stop loving me."

"I'll never stop loving you, you know that."

David leaned over and kissed Misty on the forehead.

"Different David," she said. "I'm sorry."

"No need to be sorry," he replied. "I love you for you, not for what you were, or what you might be. I don't want you to hurt yourself, but I do love you just as you are."

Misty hugged David and pulled him on top of her.

It took Misty two hours to get ready to walk out the door. She did not look her best, but she tried. She made the effort to look beautiful for David.

"How do I look?" she asked.

"You look stunning."

"I do not," she said.

"You look like the girl I love on the way to the beach where we are going to watch the sunset, swim naked in the water and screw in the surf."

Misty smiled.

"I like the way you think, David."

"You corrupted me. It took a while, but you dragged my mind right down into the gutter."

"I like it," she said. "We're both going to hell and you're riding shotgun."

David laughed. "Where have I heard that before?"

Drake was ready to take the limo, but David told him they'd take the

Packard instead. It was the easiest way for Misty not to be recognized. And if they were going to sneak off for a date at the beach they sure didn't need the limo.

They drove to Topanga Canyon and parked high up on the hill where the sun could be seen as it danced on the edge of the Pacific. David and Misty sat on the hood of the car, held hands and breathed in the fresh ocean air. The surf pounded the beach way below.

"Do you want to take a walk?" asked Misty, finally.

"Sure," said David. "I'd love to take a walk with you."

David grabbed his camera and, hand-in-hand, the two strolled on over toward the edge of the cliff. Misty posed a couple of times and David made some pictures of the late sunlight lighting up the back of her hair.

"I love doing this," said Misty. "Thank you for making me come with you."

"Nature and beauty work well together," David said. He took another picture.

"David?"

"Yes, Misty?"

"Will we always be together?"

There was a deep rumble.

Drake was on his way home after having taken the limo out to get the oil changed. He tuned the radio.

"*And repeating breaking news from the last hour. A tragic accident has occurred and the latest news is that screen star Misty Adams and celebrity photographer David Ross have been found dead at Topanga. Witnesses say they saw the couple near the edge of the cliff apparently doing a photo shoot when the ground gave way. Both were pronounced dead at the scene. Ross had been dating screen actress Misty Adams since her long awaited return to the big screen...*"

Chapter 14

December 7, 2008

Canyon Lake, Texas

Wallace had to shake Lauri to get her to come out of her trance. He snapped his fingers several times and she didn't respond. Her eyes didn't look normal and her heart was pounding so hard Wallace could see the blood vessels pulsing in her neck.

"What happened?" he asked tensely.

"I don't know," said Lauri with a panicked look on her face. "It was like I was stuck in this tunnel and couldn't get out. Things were closing in on me and I was really scared." Tears started flowing out of her eyes. She grabbed Wallace and clutched him tightly.

"It's okay," he said. "You're okay now."

"No, I'm not," she said, "I'm scared."

"You'll be all right."

Lauri squeezed him. He patted her back and held her close.

"That's the weirdest thing I've ever done," said Lauri.

"What happened?"

"I don't know. It was freaky. I was in this long tunnel and I saw Melissa, but I don't know what happened after that. I saw David, David sitting on this couch!" She patted Wallace's couch with her hand for emphasis. Lauri breathed hard. "Did you feel anything?"

"No," confirmed Wallace.

Lauri gently kissed him, and then harder.

The energy sparked and they both shared the past life experience. It was clear, then, and not at all what they expected.

"Oh, God," said Lauri finally. "It didn't work, did it?"

"I guess not," said Wallace.

"It's different, but the same in the end."

"That's okay," said Wallace, "maybe we can't change everything. Maybe we just don't know how."

"It's too scary," said Lauri.

She buried her head on his shoulder and he stroked her back. She watched the rain as it continued to hit the window.

"It's okay," he said. "We tried and when you're ready we can try again."

After a silence, Lauri whispered in Wallace's ear. "*Look for me*," she said.

"*I will find you*," said Wallace.

Chapter 15

May 1025
Dublin, Ireland

In the spring, Ireland may be the greenest place on earth. The forests were certainly plush and the streams and brooks that babbled through the trees were sent from God. The water flowed swiftly, bubbled up around rocks that protruded to the surface, and swirled around in circles. Occasionally a leaf would drop out of a tree, land on the surface of the water and be whisked away like a little boat.

Wildlife was abundant, and the days were majestic. The meadows smelled so fresh and clean as to invigorate the whole body. It had rained hard the night before and there was quite a lightning storm, but by afternoon it was starting to dry out. Tree stumps still showed signs of having taken a soaking and there were toads that sang their approval.

Dub and Meallan's children were off down the stream, playing in the water, trying to catch fish. A couple of the boys had decided to build a dam across the stream and forever stop it. They had created a pool where the girls played with glee.

Dub walked with Meallan's hand in his. The children's voices could still be heard but they were around a bend and could not be seen. They came upon a waterfall where the stream poured water into a little canyon and created a small pool. It was beautiful and sounded so peaceful.

"I have dreams," said Meallan. "Dreams that our children will grow up and have families of their own."

"And they will," said Dub. "Now that Ireland is free, they will all have families and places of their own."

"I dreamed you died in that battle," said Meallan.

"But I didn't," said Dub. "I'm still here and that was so long ago."

"I know," she said.

Dub stopped and the two looked at the brook. The sound of the water was soothing.

"What will it be like here in a thousand years?" asked Meallan.

"It will be just like this," he said. "The beauty of Ireland will always be the same."

"Will it?"

"Of course it will. Look around you. It's already been here a thousand years. Maybe ten thousand years. It will always be this way."

"What about us?"

"Us?" asked Dub.

"Do you think we will be here in a thousand years?"

Dub smiled. It was an odd question.

"I don't know," he said. "But I

can tell you one thing." He stopped and pushed Meallan up against a huge tree. He put his hand on her thigh and pushed up her dress.

Meallan breathed in.

"I can tell you one thing," he repeated.

"What's that?" said Meallan.

Dub kissed Meallan as he moved his hand. Their lips sent electricity into each others' bodies.

"I will love you for a thousand years."

Genesis of a Story

By Douglas Kirk

We didn't finish the video production the night the entity was first encountered, so we returned, this time on October 24, 2008, and part way through reciting her lines, the actress once again said she sensed the entity.

This time, though, the entity was angry, and my model got into a fight with her. The model told the entity to leave her alone, let her do her work, quit bothering her. She raised her voice to the entity out in the darkness. I thought, "Wow, I can't believe I'm witnessing this." It was the same deal as the previous contact, except that this time, the entity was apparently trying to project a sense of extreme anger. That event went on for an hour or more. All the while, I didn't see anything, despite the model's urging me to turn around, because she said the entity was appearing behind me. Finally, it subsided.

As camera people know, when it comes to wrapping a shoot, the photographer likes to pack up his own gear. I'm the same way. I want to put each item in its assigned pocket so that the next time I reach for it, it will be there. I don't want stuff jumbled, so, when people offer to help me pack up, I generally say, "No, let me do it."

That's how all my photo shoots end and my model knew that, so when I sat down to pack up all the gear, she took a seat on the ground next to her stuff to wait for me and we talked about that entity.

It was then that she looked out across the graveyard and made a statement I'll never forget. "These people aren't dead. People go on, you know."

I asked what she meant by that and so she described the concept that grave markers are simply benchmarks in a very long life. I don't think she said it in exactly those words, but that's what she got across to me.

Many of us believe in an afterlife, but what about the concept of a beforelife? Is that possible?

That is an idea that I had not really seriously considered before, but whether you believe it or not, I thought, it would make a great fictional story. Within a few days after that, I wrote some notes that became the premise of this series.

I'm not sure how, but I knew at the time, that there would be two main characters. The man would somehow be saved by the girl and he in turn, would save her. I knew from the very start that the man would be involved in a battle of some kind and that the night before he died, he'd sneak off to visit his lover and that through a bond they formed, they would go on as a couple forever.

I knew that these characters would realize that they had known each other for a thousand years, and that upon an awakening in present day, the hero would wonder how long he had been looking for her. The line he used in my scribbled notes, which is not in the book at all, was, "Tell me the name of the century, a thousand years is so wrong."

After I wrote those notes, I went over them with my friend and she encouraged me to write the story. I didn't. Instead, I let two years pass. She and I discussed the story and we discussed her belief in the possibility of reincarnation. But for some reason, I was just not ready to write the first book.

I had always wanted to write a time-travel story and have been a big fan of any book or movie that allows people to move about in time and space. In fact, as a photographer, freezing moments in time is my business, so having a device, even though it is just fictional, to unfreeze time, is pretty attractive to me.

To be continued...

Reviews

I Will Find You

Worldwide

When I read Douglas Kirk's first book in this series, I thought he was a great writer. But when I read *I Will Find You*, I changed my mind about Kirk. He's no longer just in the category of "greats." Kirk has moved into "brilliant." The second book was not a re-hash of the first. It took an amazing new direction that kept me enthralled and really got me to thinking--Kirk is not imagining this story--he really is remembering it. I could be wrong, but I'm convinced I'm right.

--Clifton Spencer, California

Splendid! *I Will Find You* has me well on the way to traveling to Ireland. I have never been so inspired in all my life. I don't know, but I wonder, is this really possible? If it is, I want to know for myself.

--Drew O'Henry, New York

Here is an example of the second book being as good as the first! It doesn't always happen, but it sure did this time! *I Will Find You* opened new doors and shed light in new areas. It not only held my attention, but kept me anxiously awaiting. I earnestly looked forward to turning the page in order to find out what was going to happen next! The only bad part was having to end the book. I truly fell deeper in love with the characters and did not want my time with them to end.

--Jamie L. Stinson, RN, MSN, Mexico

I Will Find You

I just finished reading *I Will Find You*. I thought *Look For Me* had me really captivated, but this second in the series is absolutely outstanding! I connected with the characters and I found myself wanting them to succeed in every way. I identified especially with one character, but I imagine each reader will have his or her own favorite. Douglas Kirk has done it again, in telling this story and drawing us into some amazing lives. I don't know if there's another story to follow, but there bloody well better be! I'm waiting impatiently for the next one!

--Lorraine Brandt, Texas

After reading Doug's first book, *Look For Me,* and experiencing how it lingers, I couldn't wait to read *I Will Find You.* I opened the book to read at a leisurely pace, however, as in the first one, I became so engrossed in it that there was no way of stopping. The author lures you into the story until you become so immersed in it, that you can't put the book down. Even after the last page is read the images remain with you for a long time. This is one of those books that can be read and re-read and not lose its magic. I would find two lovers connecting and just when I thought I was seeing what would tear them apart, another curve ball! The characters were true to life and it is so well-written. This past weekend I found myself picking up this book again and re-reading some parts. It was *just that good.* Such a blend of history and romance. I will read everything that becomes available from this author!

--Dodie Bernard, Canada

I was discussing this book with a fellow reader about my favorite scene in the book, where Dean is teasing Melissa in the feed store. We agreed that even though Dean is a fictional character, he must be adorable. It just goes to show how well these lovable (or despicable) characters interact with their surroundings or one another. And now I need therapy for having a crush on a fictional character.

--Natalie Cross, Colorado

Synopsis

I Will Find You

It is impossible to know the future, and a split second is just enough time to end something that offers such great hope. But then there is the discovery that maybe love can change the past.

Is there a second chance? Are there guardian angels? Can you count on reality to stay the same?

The second book in the *Look For Me* series explores a new reality.

Is it memory or imagination? That's the question Douglas Kirk kept asking himself as he wrote *Look For Me*, his first novel spanning a thousand years and two continents. A battle in eleventh century Ireland, an immigration ship in 1850, a coal mine in the 1870s, and 1950s Hollywood, these are the settings.

When he finished that book, he thought he had completed the project. He was wrong. *I Will Find You* sprang into his mind before the first book had even gotten out of editorial.

"I don't know what happened," said Kirk. "The characters were so strong and were so much a part of me that they just continued to linger. I couldn't help it. Before I knew it, I was writing the second in the series. I was a passenger in an adventure that seemed to have no limits. The possibilities were endless and my characters grabbed me and would not let me go."

An idea that was conceived two years prior to the writing of the first book was so powerful that it just continued. This time, though, the settings picked up where the others left off and Kirk found himself back in Ireland, in California in 1898, in New York during the Spanish American War and struggling to survive the 1932 dust bowl in North Texas.

"What we learned about human existence in the first book took a new twist in the second," said Kirk "and I didn't even know what was happening until the words hit the page. Can love be that strong? I think it can, and when this comes out as a motion picture, it will change the way lovers view the world."

About The Author

Douglas Kirk

Douglas Kirk has been writing all of his adult life. He is an accomplished photographer. Kirk said when he studied at the American International High School in The Hague, Holland, that he'd be happy in life if he could be a writer and photographer.

He graduated with honors from Texas A&M University with a B.S. in Psychology, an M.S. in Experimental Psychology (specializing in learning) and a B.S. in Journalism (with a minor in photography).

He's had more than 350 articles and 500 photographs published in national magazines. He owns a community newspaper that has earned 119 awards in writing and photography, including Kirk as Photojournalist of the Year for Texas from the Houston Press Club (twice), and the Vic Mauldin Memorial Award for Advertising Photography (seven times) from the Texas Community Newspaper Association. Kirk has written twenty-five other books.

The Tetralogy

Look For Me I Will Find You

Series

Look For Me sets the stage.
What a difference a little kiss made.

I Will Find You gives you a twist you won't believe.
Imagine, if love could change the past.

Missing You will blow your mind.
Who would have ever thought
love could be so strong?

Everything To Me will put you on the edge.
How could something so special go so wrong?

I Will Find You

Ordering Information

If you would like to order copies of any of the books in this series, you may do so for $9.95 each (plus $2.55 shipping and handling for one book or $3.55 shipping and handling for two to four books.) Send check or money order to:

Morton Falls Publishing Company
1850 Old Sattler Road
Canyon Lake, TX 78132

List the title and the quantity of books you would like in your letter and clearly indicate your shipping address.

Autographed copies may be purchased at:

www.LookForMeIWillFindYou.com

You may contact the author directly at:

LookForMeIWillFindYou@aol.com.

Please put the title of the book in the subject line. Due to the volume of e-mail received the author may not be able to answer directly or right away. He does appreciate your feedback and questions.

Contact Hollywood and beg them to make the motion picture series.